The Strange Case at Misty Ridge

Also by David Brian

Dark Albion

Carmilla: The Wolves of Styria

Carmilla: A Dark Fugue

The Cthulhu Child

Kaleen Rae: And Other Weird Tales

Gloop!

The Damnation Game

Big Bad

The Strange Case

at Misty Ridge

David Brian

Night-Flyer

The Strange Case at Misty Ridge

2017 David Brian

2017 Night-Flyer Publishing

ISBN-13: 978-1542503044
ISBN-10: 1542503043

First published in 2017 by Night-Flyer Publishing

This one is for Emily and Alex; it's important that you know.

"What matters isn't whether something is real. What matters is if it is true."

~Jane Mendelsohn, *innocence*

The Strange Case at Misty Ridge

Humankind is but the pieces in a game, plastic soldiers waging war between boy gods.

I have a persistent, recurring memory from my childhood. It is strange perhaps, but since the accident these are the only scenes I recall with any genuine clarity from that period.

The summer break seemed to last forever in those halcyon days. We would spend endless hours playing in fields stretching either side of The Nene. The river, cutting a swathe through my home town, was in those times a focal point for young and old alike. The more sedate areas of its bank, lined with families, enjoying days of paddling and picnics beneath cloudless skies. Farther upstream anglers cast their lines, spotted out along the bank like ants attacking a caterpillar. For our part, we preferred the wilds of the northern end of town, and what had once been the Kingsthorpe Mill. The waters flowed faster here, and the hulking remnant of the old millhouse made for an exciting base. About a half-mile north of the millhouse the river took one of its many forks, and some way beyond this diversion an overflow fed off to form a central lagoon. This area was strictly off bounds to children, partially because of the depth of the water, but also because of the numerous trolleys, old bikes, and sharp and hefty branches that had been discarded in the water. We swam in that pool almost every day of the summer.

Earlier in the day there had been perhaps fifty youngsters enjoying the cool waters of the lagoon. The ages of the assemblage probably ranged between seven and twenty, but it remained an unwritten rule from time immemorial, there was never any age related bullying. The older youths had once been our age, and they allowed us the same tolerance they previously enjoyed.

It was almost seven in the evening, and the earlier crowd had dispersed. Simon, Gerry, and I were in no rush to go anywhere. Each of us had brought along a pack-up of soda, crisps and sandwiches – and Gerry's mother delighted by including sausage rolls in the tuck; enough to feed us all. It was our intention to enjoy as much *outside time* as the holiday permitted. We sat on the lightning burnt remains of an old Oak, which had fallen to form a precarious bridge across the river's narrowest point. Laughing and reminiscing over the day's events. We tucked heartily into the pack-ups, our bare feet swishing the cool waters as we watched the orange sun slipping towards the horizon.

It was a little piece of Heaven.

As we finished up our tuck the conversation shifted to girls. It remained a mystery at that time, but Gerry was the only one of us who ever demonstrated much ability in the *pulling* department. Only some years later did I realize the secret to Gerry's success. It was a confidence thing. The kid had the foresight to carry himself well in the company of the opposite sex, unlike the majority of other eleven-year-olds, who for the most part were reduced to gibbering wrecks when confronted by girls they found even remotely interesting. For weeks Gerry had had his eye on Bev Kingston, and earlier that day most of the lads at the lagoon had eyes on the same. Bev had turned up with two girlfriends, and along with Carol Giffen, she had been persuaded to swim in the pool. Neither of them had brought swimwear, and so they swam in their undies. Bev's whites turned completely transparent within minutes of her being in the water, and certainly for those of a similar age to ourselves, it was our first experience seeing *the real deal.* The fact Gerry then plucked up courage to ask Bev for a date, and she readily agreed on a trip to the cinema with him the following night; well, major kudos points for *kid plucky.* Simon and I were almost green with envy, and Gerry was intent on milking his achievement for all it was worth.

So there we sat, our feet hanging in the steady current, enjoying a time of life that is meant to be enjoyed.

Simon started, and suddenly he was pointing westwards, in the direction of the railway arches supporting the tracks leading from Northampton Station. To this day, I can still recall his words, and the raised pitch twisting his voice into that of a stranger. His tone excitable as a child's on Christmas morning, tainted not by fear, but strained and racing like the accelerated ramblings of a boy who has evaded a chasing dog.

"Oh. My. God. Do you see that?"

I raised an open palm to my brow, shielding my eyes from horizontal spears of sunlight. "Do I see what?"

"Do you see that?" Gerry said, reiterating Simon's question, his finger wavering excitedly as he pointed across open fields, towards the railway bridges.

I squinted my eyes some more and tried again to focus in on whatever so excited my friends. "I can't se –" My jaw slackened. "Jesus… I think that's a –"

"It's a panther, right?" Simon said. "It's a bloody black panther."

"Holy crap!" Gerry was fidgeting as though he had ants crawling in his pants, the nervous excitement almost enough for him to lose his seating on the trunk.

"Careful," I said. "You'll end up in the drink if you don't keep still."

"But it's a *big cat!*"

"I can see that. But keep the noise down; otherwise it'll know we're here." Of course, my words were nonsense. The animal couldn't know we were there. But I didn't want to risk spooking the creature. I wasn't sure if its getting wind of our presence would result in it fleeing, or entice it to come hunting for us…

The animal was perhaps two-hundred meters distant, we watched as it moved down the bank away from the railway tracks. It disappeared from view briefly, losing itself among thick foliage at the foot of the slope, before reappearing and continuing to move parallel with the bank, edging the unlabored field, the beast pressed on towards the railway arches. We watched in awe as its black body slinked through grasses as high as its shoulder, and with whispered exchanges we agreed the animal was comparable in size to a leopard – the only place any of us had ever seen a leopard was during a school trip to London Zoo, but this creature, although smaller than a lion, was far larger than an Alsatian dog, and would have been a veritable giant alongside a household moggy. It *had* to be a leopard of some sort: A panther.

The beast moved with abandon, seeming almost leisurely as it proceeded onwards. The railway arches bridged another branch of The Nene, and it occurred to me that maybe the animal was heading for the shallows beneath the bridge. The overhanging shade served to keep this stretch of water cool, and maybe the cat intended taking a drink?

Simon was wearing a troubled expression. "I don't think it is a panther, or a leopard, or anything like that."

I gave him my best doubting look. "What are you talking about? Look at the size of the thing!"

"I know. It's big. But look at the shape of it. A panther should be longer in the body than that. And the tail doesn't look right, either. A panther would have a longer tail than that. I know it's a massive cat but, shape wise, it more closely resembles a *regular* cat."

Cocoa appeared in my mind's eye, the jet black cat whose licks and mews greeted my every morning. Then I thought about the leopard I'd seen in the zoo. Simon was right. The animal was without doubt a big cat, but the look of this creature didn't quite fit the image of either of those animals. To the right of the arches, an abundance of thick bushes obstructed our view of the beast's final approach towards *The Beach.*

The stretch of land we referred to as The Beach – a local name attributed to it by generations of townsfolk – was a fifty-meter long, twenty-meter deep embankment of soft soil along the waters to the right of the railway arches. The Beach wasn't laid with sand, but the bed was a mix of hard clay, layered with particles of smooth, predominantly white rock. To all intents and purposes, it was as close to a beach as you'd ever find along the river bank.

The cat had disappeared among the shrubs right of The Beach. For some minutes we waited, our eyes searching for any movement among the foliage that might alert us to the animal's reemergence.

"Holy shit!"

"What?" Simon and I asked in unison.

Gerry climbed to his feet, his arm once again pointing, this time directly at The Beach. "There's a girl."

"What?" again we responded as a duet.

"A girl… There's a naked girl on The Beach. I just saw her. She's headed down to the water."

"Bullshit!" Simon said. "You're telling me you've seen two naked girls in one day?"

"Forget that," I said. "It's not important. Think about it, Simon. If there is somebody over at the river; girl, or not; naked, or not, there's a sodding black leopard headed straight in their direction."

"Oh crap… what do we do?"

"Only one thing we can do," Gerry said, scooting along the trunk and back onto the bank. He picked up the thickest stick he could find laying on the ground. "You two coming?" he asked.

"Are you crazy? It's dangerous," I said.

"Yep, it most probably is. So then, are you two pussies coming, or what?"

Moments later we were tearing across unlabored fields, armed with wholly inadequate weapons. We had chosen the firmest, most solid branches we could find as our staffs, each of us having the foresight to select a piece of wood with an end broken to form a point. We ran headfirst towards the unknown, but we weren't completely gullible. We ran together, Simon to my right, and Gerry to the left of me, never once allowing our stride to separate us by more than an arm's length, intent on making ourselves look a cohesive and daunting target for any animal (particularly any black panthers) that fell into our path. The second part of our plan involved noise, and even before we were within a hundred meters of The Beach, or the wild undergrowth set to its right, we began yelling and screaming. We hoped that our warning might serve to alert whoever it was Gerry had spied moving down to the water, but mayhap the girl was distracted – and for sure there was a girl, and a stunningly attractive figure she presented – for we were perhaps less than sixty meters from water's edge when her slim frame appeared over the lip of The Beach – the point where rough field falls away to a pretense of sand. This placed the girl within forty meters of our position, and in shocked unison we fell silent, our forward momentum grinding to a halt.

It was only a momentary loss of focus, although to each of us it applied – of that much I am sure. The girl had hair as black as coal; hanging loose about her shoulders, its length enough to partially obscure pert breasts. She was perhaps eighteen, certainly no older, but still qualified as *a woman* to us. I was mesmerized; the luster of her body betrayed the fact she had indeed entered those waters beneath the arches, and I watched as droplets ran down her belly and settled amid that glistening, wispy triangle. For an instant – and it was only one fleeting moment – our eyes made contact. Even from some distance it was impossible not to notice just how green her eyes were, although equally striking was the graveness of her features. I wondered if perhaps she had seen the cat – and then I remembered *the cat!*

I had recovered my senses, suddenly remembering why we were there. Perhaps it was with too much vigor, but I exploded into warning: "The cat! Watch out there's a bleeding great leopard somewhere in those bushes!" I gesticulated like a wild thing. "Seriously, lady, get your clothes on and get away from there!"

My words acted as a spur to my friends, and suddenly three lunatic boys were screaming like maniacs at a stunned and naked young woman. She took a backwards step, and it occurred to me that our behavior was perhaps frightening her more than any concerns over an alleged giant animal. She turned and fled down towards the water.

"Wait!" I begged, already in hot pursuit.

"We have to stop her," I heard Simon at my heels. "The panther could be down there."

The three of us reached the lip almost together, falling to a halt as our jaws fell open.

The panther was two thirds of the way across the strait by the time we settled on the lip, it's smooth and steady strokes allowing it to all but glide through the water. The naked girl was gone. She was nowhere in sight, even though the buildup of foliage near where she had stood would have prevented her exiting in that direction, and if she had moved towards the arches she would still be in our view.

"What the fuck?" Gerry's words summed up the situation perfectly.

"Jesus Christ, I think it's chased her across the river," Simon said.

I looked at him and pondered how someone with such impressive grades could be so dumb. "No chance. She couldn't have swum across that quickly. Besides, look at how thick the bracken is over there. Where would she go?

Gerry nodded. "I think Jack's right. She had nowhere to go." He pointed to the cat, which had all but completed its swim. "Do you know what I'm thinking? Remember that book we found in the library last year, the one on weird creatures? It talked about such animals. History is full of 'em. These days it's all about werewolves. It's all werewolves this, werewolves that – you know what I'm saying, right?"

Across the river the black cat was coming up onto the bank. It stopped and turned towards us, seemingly fixing its big green eyes on me. And in that moment I was sure I had looked into those same eyes once before. And then it was gone, turning and swiftly disappearing into the thick undergrowth.

"That wasn't like any sort of leopard I've ever seen," Gerry muttered.

I nodded, opening my mind to impossibility.

"Sounds like Gerry's making crazy talk," Simon said.

I made a sweeping gesture with my arm. "So where did the girl go, Simon? Where did she go, eh?"

He shook his head. "I don't know... but perhaps we should get out of here."

"Not yet," Gerry said, skipping down the embankment towards the water's edge.

I called after him. "What are you doing?"

"Looking for paw prints. And footprints. If you're coming down, watch where you're treading. Don't stomp over any potential evidence."

I joined him at the water's edge and we spent a few minutes squatting in various spots, trying to identify prints belonging to either the girl or the panther. I was just about to suggest we give up when I noticed Simon farther along the bank; close to the area we first lost sight of the black cat. He was standing with his back straight, but appeared to be staring at something on the ground.

"Are you okay?" I called.

"Erm, lads, I think I may have found something."

We hurried to join Simon, who was standing in a mud bank, and then we looked on in awe, staring wide-eyed at the set of paw prints that proved beyond any doubt we had witnessed a huge cat in the English countryside. But those pads weren't the revelation, because placed directly in front of them, as though walking the same line was a set of bare, human footprints. Judging from the size, they appeared to belong to a female.

"Look," said Simon. "These are definitely prints from that cat. But it's muddy all around here, so where are the rest of its prints? If it had jumped to clear the mud then there'd be deeper indentations at some point, but there isn't. Where did it go?"

Gerry pointed to the human prints. "There," he said. "That's where it went."

The sun was setting, and already the evening was growing dull. None of us commented directly, but I am certain there wasn't one of us wanted to be in those fields after dark. The next day we would meet up to discuss the things we had seen, and *the cat* would end up being a regular topic of conversation over the next several months, until, finally, its vividness began to diminish, and the whole incident seemed less important.

However, on that first night we saw the animal, I'd hardly been able to get home quickly enough, as I wanted to tell my parents about the strange occurrence we had witnessed.

The reaction to our discovery was disappointing. It didn't receive anything like the adulation I felt it deserved.

My father laughed. 'I think your imagination is playing tricks on you, son. Or maybe you have a touch of heat stroke? Best you keep out of those beams for the next few days, eh?' It was the response I should have expected.

Neither of my parents had been raised in *money* families, but as a couple they'd been fairly successful buying up old properties, doing them up then selling them on. I had little memory of these events, presumably because I was a youngster at the time, but according to my sisters, my parents had once renovated a two-hundred year-old, three storied sandstone dwelling, standing in dereliction at the heart of the village of Old; events at Madeline Cottage had cut a deep scar into my family's history, the place supposedly being subject to some very odd phenomena; hence my father's later tendency towards discrediting anything suggestive of the otherworldly. As I said previously, I remembered little to nothing of either the building or the alleged events therein, but even my elder sisters tended to shy away from discussing our time spent there. I have to admit, any mention of that place still gives me unexplained chills.

Mother had proven a little more supportive with regards to the cat, although she too offered little validation. She inclined towards our having misinterpreted the scene, suggesting that what we may actually have witnessed was a normal cat, but its distant image somehow being expanded by the rays of the setting sun. Like a desert mirage.

Yeah, right. Thanks, Mom and Dad.

By the end of the week I'd learned not to bother mentioning the incident when at home. My parents were bad enough, but having two sisters who relished every opportunity of making my life hell...the cat incident quickly became a weapon of ridicule. So I tucked it safely away in a little memory box; although I never forgot about it. Even following on from the accident, in those dark days when I'd forgotten most everything else; I never forgot *the cat.*

Two

I watch in terror as a thick muscled arm rises from beneath the surface of the gooey pool, and I am certain She has summoned my death.

It's been almost thirty years since I encountered the cat; and a little more than seven since I survived the accident that changed everything. I guess the nature of that second incident meant there were always going to be long-term repercussions, and, to be honest given the circumstances, I've always considered myself lucky just being here...although, even more so than the long-term damage inflicted on my health, it was the other *event* that truly changed my perception of reality.

Each morning I would open my eyes, regardless of whether being greeted by the sound of a dawn chorus, with sunlight spotlighting through the drapes, highlighting motes dancing in the air about me; or perhaps outside the rain was falling heavily, offering naught save window light that is dog wash gray; either way, it all seemed good to me, because I had come to view each and every morning as a victory.

Each and every day was *life.*

Let's be honest, it's a fact most of us learn only too well, and usually early on; just when you think things are going swell… life gets sucky. Well, here's the truth as I'd always seen it; you just better pick yourself up, dust yourself down, *embrace the suck* and move on. Until recently I would have told you that's a lesson worth remembering. Because I'm sounding quite positive, right? But that's not to say depression hadn't already scored some home runs along the way. Hell, at times during my recovery, it clobbered the snot out of me. But it didn't matter, because I had too many good things in my life to ever truly give up fighting.

For eighteen months following the accident my emotions remained in flux, so I guess it was a good thing I'd always been a stubborn S.O.B.

Thankfully my head got sorted. That's not to say I didn't still have times when I suffered. On any given day I could be found loitering between mild discomfort and severe pain, and on those worst days I'd slip enough meds to date-rape a horse.

I sometimes wondered if I was an addict.

I also pondered if it was the drugs I was taking accounted for any of the weird shit I'd experienced.

Oh, if only that were the case.

Before I begin in earnest, I should mention Linda, my partner of twenty-three years, and wife for the last twenty of those. She's a damn lucky woman…but then I would say that, right? Seriously though, she is my rock, my soulmate and my world, and without her love and support I doubt I could ever have made it through any of my previous traumas. I love everything about the woman; although I will say this, it is Linda's willingness to support my crazy-ass interests that has landed me in half of the trouble I regularly find myself in. It is also Linda who has supplied the strength to pull me through these same trials. You don't believe me? Well then, I suggest you read on.

One final point, with regards all of the positive anecdotes espoused here; don't read too much into any of that. Because, given the nature of recent events, I can only pray that in time I am able to rediscover such a mindset. If I've learned anything over these past few weeks, it's to not rule out the very real possibility that Hell exists.

Three

These terrible things I have seen...such horrors experienced.

I had always held affection for the paranormal, even prior to my childhood escapades with the panther and the naked girl. I grew up fascinated by stories of bizarre creatures and events, but the cat incident fired my interest in things unexplained to new heights. Over the following years I amassed a sizeable collection of literature, and collected an equally large selection of newspaper clippings, articles and photographs of anything to do with the unexplained, ranging from UFO's, to crop circles and ghosts. However, married life, and a job in the electrical construction industry, meant that over the course of time my *hobby* got placed firmly on the backburner, and the accumulated books and cuttings were eventually packed away in boxes, and placed up in the loft.

Four years ago I was on the way to a solid recovery, although still somewhat prone to bouts of depression. Linda suggested that perhaps, as I now had free time on my hands, I should consider rededicating myself to some paranormal research; possibly with a view to using any evidence I uncovered as source material for writing a book – the book still hasn't happened yet.

It took very little consideration before deciding it was a solid idea. I ordered some business cards online, and placed an advertisement in one of the local free papers. I advertised my services as Keswick Investigations. Linda wasn't sure about the name as she felt it made me sound like a detective agency, and Mother agreed with her; although my mother was totally opposed to my meddling with *dark forces,* so her protestations over the choice of name were discounted. Anyhow, I was in agreement that it sounded somewhat officious, but personally I liked that. So the name stayed.

So here I am today, working from home, using the spare bedroom at the back of our three-bedroom, red-brick semi as a makeshift office. It's ideal really, as long as I never need to swing a cat in here. Seriously, they market these rooms as bedrooms? I don't even know how house builders get away with it. It's a blatant contravention of the trade description act.

Anyway, enough of my continual whining, the room serves its purpose just fine. There is barely space to accommodate a desk, computer and filing cabinet, but I have also managed to slot in a couple of chairs, just in case any potential clients call around – this is a rarity, but it does happen.

That's about it really, things have been going well. In just four years, I have investigated fourteen cases of haunting, of which three involved poltergeists; two exorcisms, twenty UFO sightings; reports of a strange slime-monster sighted up by the old Danish encampment; a woman claiming to have been impregnated by a vampire; three cases of alien abduction, and an alleged werewolf attack. Seriously, I'm not even joking about the werewolf.

So, it's fair to say I have experience involving a wide variety of paranormal activity; some of which has been pretty mundane, and one or two cases that have been downright bloody creepy. However, all of this pales into insignificance when compared to my latest case, the events of which have upset me greatly, and quite probably left an impression on my psyche that I may never recover from.

It started on a morning much like any other morning. It was a Wednesday, just over three weeks ago. I was upstairs in my office, going over witness reports of unidentifiable craft. More than forty witnesses had reported seeing these strange triangular objects flying above the Thames Valley the previous week. To be honest I wasn't in the best of moods (I know, I'm coming across as a dour sod, right?). The latch on the back window was broken; which meant I couldn't let any air into the room, and even though it was still only mid-morning, the June heat wave inexplicably spreading across the country was making my morning unbearable.

I wasn't expecting company, so when I heard the doorbell ring, quickly followed by the sound of Linda in the hallway, and then another female voice, I assumed it was one of her girlfriends dropping by for coffee.

It was only as I heard footfalls on the stairwell, it occurred to me that maybe it was I who had a visitor. I glanced at the open diary lying on my desktop, and this confirmed what I already knew; I had no appointments booked.

My wife stopped as she reached the doorway and gestured her companion to enter the room. Experience had taught her my office was far too snug to accommodate more than a couple of people comfortably. Linda smiled as the woman edged slowly past her.

"Jack, this is Mrs. Featherstone. She hasn't got an appointment, but I really think you'll want to hear what she's got to say."

"Thanks, luv," I said, before turning my attention to the unexpected visitor. "So, Mrs. Featherstone, just what may I do for you, on this fine day?"

The attempted brevity seemed lost on the woman. Instead, she proceeded to shuffle hesitantly into the room, head slightly bowed, like a monk in contemplation. She walked with drooping shoulders, as though her arms were weighed down with bags of heavy shopping.

"Mr. Keswick, please forgive the intrusion. I am sure you're a very busy man, but I have come some way to see you today. My family and I really need your help. Please say you will help us?"

The strained tones of her voice were enough to convince me she was genuine, at least in her belief that my services may be of use. Her hair was jet black, styled in a striking wedge-cut. She had wide brown eyes, although her sockets were reduced to dark bags. I was looking at an extremely tired and worn down young woman. Despite her appearance she was not unattractive, and the pale-blue dress she wore adequately showed off a pencil slim figure. She was barely into her mid-twenties, and it occurred to me I had rarely seen such angst, and never before displayed by one so young.

"Take a seat," I gestured, drawing up one of the spare chairs alongside the desk.

"Thank you." She lowered herself into the seat. "Mr. Keswick, can you help me?"

"I'm sure that I can," I replied, trying my best to sound reassuring. "But perhaps you should start by telling me everything, from the very beginning."

"It's difficult…I know it's happening, but when I say it aloud it sounds crazy," she said, the hesitance straining her chords.

I leaned in closer to her and smiled what I hoped was a reassuring smile. "Mrs. Featherstone, I very much doubt there is *anything* that you could say to me which would be any stranger than some of the things I have seen and heard before. I consider myself to be a very good judge of character, and I can tell that something is genuinely troubling you. So, please, don't be embarrassed. Anything you tell me here today is strictly confidential, okay?"

"Okay," she nodded, perhaps more confidently. "My husband, Mark, and I live in Claybrooke. It's a quaint little village about twenty-eight miles north of here, across the Leicestershire border. I don't suppose you know it?"

I shook my head. "Sorry, I've never had the pleasure, but I'm sure it's lovely."

"It is," she beamed. "We were very lucky. Mark's brother works as a loss adjuster for one of the major building societies. He knew we were looking to buy a place in the countryside, and so when he heard about this beautiful little thatched cottage that was being repossessed because of a default on the mortgage, well, he tipped us off. A bit naughty, I know, but he was only trying to help us get a good start on the ladder."

I shrugged my shoulders. "Fair play to you, there's nothing wrong with snatching up a bargain."

"Exactly," she acquiesced in her overly anxious way, as though relieved to have my support. "Anyway, Misty Ridge – our cottage, that's its name – it is… it was, beautiful."

"Go on." I urged.

She took a couple of deep breaths, composing herself before continuing. "In the first twelve months that we were there, we decorated inside and out. We were desperate to put our own stamp on the property. By the time the first year was up we had the place looking stunning. All of our friends and family loved it. We painted the exterior shutters white, and had the thatched roof repaired, while inside we decorated each room in pastel shades. It was perfect. I didn't think things could get any better, but then they did…"

She let out a sigh, and her upper body seemed almost to deflate as she melted back in the chair. She forced a weak smile, one that remained painted across her features as she sat silently, her thoughts adrift in some far off place.

I waited a few moments before speaking: Mrs. Featherstone. Are you okay?"

"Sorry," she said, starting. "My thoughts were somewhere else. I find that happens a lot lately… I should continue. When I was fifteen, Mr. Keswick –"

"Please," I interrupted, "call me Jack."

"Okay." She smiled. "When I was fifteen, Jack, I got cancer; it was ovarian cancer to be precise. Anyhow, I got better, but they told me I would never be able to have children. But you know what? Turns out they were wrong – because years later I got pregnant. And even though the doctors told me there was only a ten percent chance of my being able to carry the baby to full term, they were wrong about that as well. Jacob, my son, was born fit and healthy, weighing in at just over eight pounds. I had the perfect husband, the perfect child, and a perfect home."

Tears began welling in her eyes even as she talked, and very soon they were trickling down pale cheeks. I reached for the tissue box on top of my desk.

"Take your time," I soothed, passing her the box. "There's no hurry, just tell me in your own time."

The girl pulled a tissue free and dabbed at her eyes. "I'm sorry," she muttered.

"It's okay," I reassured her. "How about if I get Linda to stick the kettle on, you look like a nice cuppa might cheer you up?"

"You're very kind," she said, "but honestly, I'm fine. I would prefer to just continue if that's okay?"

"Of course," I reiterated, "whenever you feel ready."

Yet again she took some time to gather her emotions, but finally she straightened her back and gripped hold the arms of the chair. "Right," she said, "I think I'm ready to go on now."

I smiled. "Good. Just take whatever time you need, okay?"

She returned my smile. "Thank you. For the first eighteen months after Jacob was born, everything was perfect. Mark got a promotion at work – which more than made up for the fact I was now a full time mother – and we had this perfect little person sharing our lives. We were a family. Life was great…but then it started."

"Go on," I urged, leaning forward in my chair.

The girl was visibly shaking, but she continued speaking.

"It began with the voices … as I said before; Mark had gotten a promotion at work, the downside of which was that he had to work the nightshift two weeks a month. It didn't unduly bother me, being alone at night I mean, or at least it didn't at first. Then, one night, I woke to the sound of voices coming from downstairs. I was absolutely terrified. I thought there were burglars in the house, so I crept into Jacob's room; scooped him up into my arms, hurried back into my bedroom and bolted the door."

"Did you call the police?" I asked.

"No, we don't have a phone in the house."

"A cell phone, surely?"

She shook her head. "No."

"Really? So what happened next?"

"Nothing," she said. "At least nothing more that night, but my hearing voices became a regular occurrence."

"Are they male or female?" I asked.

"The voices can be male or female. Sometimes they are just talking, sometimes they are shouting, and sometimes the female voice is crying ... but the worst sound is the baby."

"The baby... there's a baby?"

"Yes, there is, or at least it's a very young child. And when it cries, well, let's just say it is really unsettling."

I liked the young woman sitting alongside me. There was innocence about her character, and she gave off a certain vibe, at least to me, that suggested she was a very genuine, caring person. But now, more than ever, she had my sympathy. Eight months ago, I dealt with a case involving a dead three-year-old. A number of the boy's family and friends had seen and spoken to him, since his death. I had found it to be a highly disturbing case to be involved with. So, if Mrs. Featherstone's family *were* being haunted, and one of the spirits was that of an infant, then they were definitely in need of my help. "Apart from the voices and other sounds, is there anything else?"

She had been chewing nervously at her top lip, but my question snapped her mind back into focus.

"Oh yes," she said, "lots else. It was about three days after the voices first began, that's when things got really bad. I would come down in the morning to find all the furniture had been re-arranged. I would always move it back into its rightful places, but then I'd leave the room for a few minutes and everything would get moved again. Then some pictures I had hung were torn from the walls, every one of them smashed to pieces. And lately, every time I set a bath running, the taps get turned off. Much like the lights in the house really, sometimes when I turn them on, someone or something else turns them off. Other times when I turn them off, within minutes they'll turn back on. Finally, this last month, well you won't believe this... I live there and I can barely believe it, but they keep painting the walls."

By this stage my head was buzzing with excitement. This definitely sounded like genuine poltergeist activity.

"So, they, the spirits, are just splashing paint randomly onto the walls, or are they writing messages?" I had just wanted to clarify exactly what she meant ... her reply blew me away.

She shook her head.

"No, they are not splashing paint on the walls. They are *painting the walls*. You know, like a decorator would."

I was speechless; I have seen and heard many very strange things over the last few years. Of course, the goings on with the lighting could have been due to an electrical fault of some kind, but ghosts helping out with the decorating?

"How does your husband feel about what is going on?" I asked.

She shook her head timidly, and again began to cry.

"I think I'm losing him. We used to be so happy, and now all we do is argue all the time. Being by myself during the night never used to scare me, but I was never really happy about Mark having to work the nightshift. I'm sure he thinks all of this is just some mad scheme of mine to make him stay home with me. I just want my husband to know that I love him, and that I'm not insane. Please, will you help me, Jack?"

We continued talking for a further forty minutes, and I was intrigued by everything that the dour Mrs. Featherstone told me. She knew much about the history of the cottage; it dated back almost two hundred years. Before her family bought it, it had belonged to another young couple, but they had no children. Before them, an old spinster had occupied the house for over sixty years, so again, no children. If I was going to get to the bottom of this, then it looked as though it would take some serious investigation.

Young Mrs. Featherstone clasped her hands together gleefully and proceeded to thank me three times over as I announced that, although busy with a prior engagement the following day, I would make it my business to visit her home at the earliest, mutually convenient opportunity.

We agreed I should visit the cottage the following Saturday. I suggested a morning appointment, as this would allow me plenty of time to carry out preliminary investigations at the family's home. It would also afford me the opportunity to interview Mr.

Featherstone. I was sure the woman was genuine, at least insofar her assessment of events occurring, but it was just possible that her husband may have a more rational explanation for what his wife perceived to be paranormal activity. Whatever the eventual truth of the matter, it was my obligation to cover every possibility.

Four

Life is an oceanic ball of possibilities, wherein, and given enough time, the tide of history seeks to repeat its flow.

Once Mrs. Featherstone had left, I went into the kitchen where I found Linda busily rolling out pastry as she listened to an overly austere newscaster on the radio. She was in the process of producing one of her wonderful corn beef tarts, which are – in my humble opinion – likely the best tasting tarts in the world. I admit this is something of an irrelevant fact, at least as far as this particular story goes, but the missus deserves credit for her outstanding culinary ability.

Resting my cane against the unit, I leaned back against the worktop, folded my arms and looked at my wife. The end of her nose was sprinkled with white powder.

"What?" she said, giving me her best disgruntled growl.

I touched a finger to my own nose. "Been on the *Charlie* again, have we?" I smirked.

She stopped rolling the pastry and walked over to me, rubbing the end of her nose gently against mine. "No, I couldn't afford any coke, so I thought I'd try sniffing flour instead."

"Well, thanks for sharing, honeybee."

"Are you hearing this?" she said, gesturing towards the radio bulletin.

"It's all sounding very grim. What's happened?"

"Another mass shooting, this time in Brussels. Fifteen dead. Plus a car bomb has just gone off in the center of Paris. Unconfirmed number of casualties, but expecting heavy losses."

"Jesus. The world has gone fricking mad."

Linda grimaced, brown eyes vibrant with anxiety. "These two attacks take the number of hits on Europe to seven in the last three weeks, and all on capital cities."

I met her gaze. "Definitely sounds like coordinated assaults."

"It's crazy."

"Of course it's crazy. If only people would take a moment and consider the bigger picture, eh? But we strike at them, and then they strike at us, ad infinitum. Pointless madness."

"So, what did you think" Linda said, her features creasing with concern.

"About these attacks?"

"About the case."

"Honestly, I really don't know quite what to think."

"I only spoke with her for a few minutes, when she first turned up at the front door, but she seemed quite serious about it all. And if even half of the things she claims are happening…"

"I know, Linz. If these events are happening in the manner she says, this could be huge."

I knew my wife's next question even before she asked it. "Jack, do you think you should call Violet in to do a reading?"

The query induced a smile. Violet Day is a clairvoyant medium, and I have been calling on her services for the past two years. I met her by chance at a paranormal convention, and she is without a doubt, *the* most gifted psychic I have ever had the good fortune to meet. She is, however, very loud, and in every sense of the word. Violet is, to put it politely, a *big* girl, a size twenty at least would be my guess, even though she stands barely five feet tall. She also has a big voice. Every word she utters literally booms out of her; which is fine for a short while, but too much time in the woman's company can be somewhat migraine inducing. With a dress sense that can be equally unsettling – she has flame-red hair, but her preference when working tends towards loose fitting clothing, and the principal choice tends to a pick from her wardrobe of swirling blue or violet caftans.

It's not a great look.

Nevertheless, Linda does tend to worry about some of the situations I have found myself in, and she seems to view Violet as some sort of psychic superhero, who has the power to keep me safe from nasty *things that go bump in the night.* Sliding my arm around Linda's trim waist, I pulled her closer, gently kissing her powdered nose.

"No honey," I said, "I'm not calling Violet in, at least, not yet."

"But, Jack –"

"No." I insisted. "I'm not calling Violet, not until I know for definite there is something for her to do."

"But you needed her at the Dresden house, and this seems like it could be as bad as, or even worse than that."

Ice melted down my spine when Linda mentioned the Dresden case. It had been almost eighteen months, but still it made my blood run cold. We had been called in to deal with the spirit of an old man who, it was alleged, had been inappropriately touching Carol Dresden, a single mother of two living in Coventry.

To be honest with you, the whole thing seemed a bit suspect; at least this was our initial impression. We had made two prior calls to what was a neat, three-bedroom brownstone terrace on the outskirts of the city, and had failed to pick up any signs of there being an occupying presence. There was no change to either the electro-magnetic, or temperature readings while we were at the house and Violet had been unable to detect any viable energies.

As was the norm, I set up various measuring gauges and meters, intending to leave them at the Dresden home for seventy-two hours. Six hours after we left, Carol called me, screaming hysterically and begging rapid assistance. She claimed that *the presence* had destroyed all of our equipment.

To say the phone call annoyed me would be a major understatement. I was convinced Carol Dresden was suffering some sort of mental issue, and that she was just using us as a means of support; perhaps to give her the attention she was seeking. Nevertheless, I had set up over two grand's worth of electronic equipment in her home, and the thought of *any* of this kit being damaged, let alone *all of it destroyed*, upset me greatly.

Two hours after receiving Carol's telephone call, Violet and I arrived back at the house, intent on giving the woman a more severe interview, and trying to find out exactly what, if anything was really going on. As Carol opened the front door and invited us to enter her home, a wooden, stand-alone coat rack suddenly flew across the hallway, striking me firmly in the chest, knocking me off of my feet.

I reached for my cane, which had spilled from my left hand as I fell, and struggled to hoist myself up from the floor. I noticed that the two women beside me were staring, open mouthed, at the goings on in the adjoining living room. Furniture was being inexplicably scooped in the air by some unseen force, hovering a few feet above the floor. And then, even as we watched, wide eyed and open mouthed, objects began flying wildly about the place. We ducked in unison as a rather hefty armchair was hurled clear of the room, clattering solidly against the wall behind us. From upstairs came the cries of Carol's two young daughters, as furniture was dragged and upended in the bedrooms above. By this time Carol was becoming hysterical, and as Violet attempted to comfort her I hobbled for the stairs. My efforts in climbing the stairs seemed to take an age, but when finally I reached the girls' room... well, I shall never, ever forget the sight that greeted me as I entered the bedroom. The girls were kneeling on one of the beds, screaming and frantically clinging to each other as the bed rocked and bucked beneath them; its metal frame a wild mustang, attempting to unseat two riders from its duvet saddle. I lurched across the room, grabbing the older girl by her wrist while urging that she didn't lose hold of her sister. I ushered the screaming children from the room, and they had reached the bottom of the stairs before I cleared the landing. As I placed my foot on the top step, the house lights began flashing like pale emergency beacons. There followed mini explosions as bulbs popped with violence enough to send tiny splinters of glass flying all around. Needless to say, we all left the property immediately, heading straight to Violet's house, which was the closest point of refuge.

Carol and her daughters stayed with Violet for the rest of that night, and when I returned the next morning Violet told me she was in contact with a retired priest named Father O'Dowd. Apparently she had known him for over twenty years, and more importantly, he had spent several years acting as chief assistant to the senior exorcist in the Catholic Church.

That evening, Linda invited Carol and her daughters around to our house for supper. Meanwhile, I returned to the Dresden home accompanied by Violet and Father O'Dowd.

The priest performed a full exorcism, with Violet acting as his assistant. While this was going on, I stood in one corner of the room, shaking with fear and silently praying to any particular deity prepared to listen – I just wanted to make it through these proceedings alive.

Three hours later, and after some very spectacular, albeit terrifying poltergeist activity, the priest's work was done and the house was cleansed. Within days Carol called in a home renovation company and arranged to have all of the damage repaired. She then put the house on the market, selling it quickly but at a knockdown price. Since that night, when we all fled in panic from her home, Carol has never once stepped back inside the property. She even arranged for some of her relatives to return and pack up all of the family's belongings.

A new family moved into the house about four months after the exorcism was carried out, and some discreet investigations confirmed they are very happy there. Nothing untoward has occurred.

Linda was staring intently at the horror written on my face. It was a look she recognized. She knew I was recalling incidents at the Dresden house.

"So, you *are* calling Violet, then?"

I shook my head.

"No. I told you, I'm not going to call her until I know there's definitely something for her to do. Besides, she's still up in Manchester until a week on Thursday. She has a lot to do sorting her aunt's estate."

Linda remained unhappy about my decision to deal with the case alone, but I promised her that if there was any *real* poltergeist activity occurring at the house, then I would just monitor the situation until I could get Violet in to assist. This seemed to put her mind at rest... somewhat.

Five

The cool desert breeze presses on my face as I stand atop the roof terrace. My eyes search the darkness beyond lights which emanate from an abundance of flat roofed dwellings. Below me, narrow streets murmur with late evening vendors, beggars and occasional tourists. In the distance, to my right, there is a large grove, the canopy of the trees rises and falls rhythmically, waves carried by an ocean of opacity. Off to my left, I see the white-stone archway which hangs over the main route into town, greeting new arrivals to Foum Zguid. Beyond this marker of civilization, the road slips into an obscurity of Moroccan night.

I turn my attention to the voices behind me. There are eight of them sharing a late meal. The restraints of their beliefs would suggest the gathering includes two couples. Their conversation, for the most part, appears relaxed, although on occasion it is broken with long periods of silence, or stern and uneven words. There is one particular woman, she sits with her back to me, but every now and again, she turns. Wet brown eyes looking in this direction, but she does not see me.

She cannot see me.

She never sees me.

Although, somehow, she senses a presence... she knows something is here.

Since the accident, and the awakening within me of this bizarre faculty, I have traveled to many places. However, I have been to this dwelling previously, perhaps approaching a half-dozen times, and although I do not know why this town, or indeed this house in particular calls to me, I feel it is this woman who draws me here.

Existence is an ocean of possibilities played out on the tidal surface of a ball. Time is not a snake that chases its own tail, but it is still possible to fully traverse the circumference of the sphere.

I move towards the group. My stride is easy; in this state of being, I no longer require a stick in my left hand in order to stand upright. I move freely, and unhindered.

As I circle the table I realize she is the only member of the gathering refraining from the conversation. She sits in silence, her covered head bowed; abstaining even when warm words are exchanged among the group. When finally she lifts her head, her eyes glisten with the pain of denial. I am overcome with the need to understand, and so I close the distance between us. I have no idea what drives me, but I choose to trace my fingers over her shoulder; she feels my touch, and this time, when she turns around, she sees me, and instantly I understand all.

The woman's name is Aya.

With just that one touch, images from Aya's mind begin overwhelming me, consuming me, becoming memories, my memories; the uncomfortable excitement of a life blossoming within my swollen belly, the care showered by a loving husband, as together we prepare for the arrival of family life; our beautiful boy, and the joy expressed on Mehdi's features that first time I introduce him to his son; but then the marks that appear over our child's body, even before little Ayoub has taken his first steps; sallow faced physicians, wringing their hands and woefully shaking their heads; and, then, chanting family members, washing then wrapping our boy in linen as white as their own bone-robes, until, finally, he is placed in the ground, his resting place encompassed amid a halo of twigs and myrtle, between wailing appeals that angels guide his journey home.

I reel from the pain of loss, but there is no respite for this damaged soul; Mehdi is a spouse whose own sorrow has turned him from loving partner to vindictive accuser, the embrace of a shared sorrow is denied me, and the only words the man can find are laced with venom. I understand it is grief that fires him, but inside I am little more than a husk, laden by the loss of a child, and now, by Mehdi too. I choose to embrace the sin of my own demise.

Mehdi has been gone for hours, this seems to be the norm these days, but regardless, he will not be returning anytime soon, and even when he does he will not mourn for me. I sit on the bed, wet eyes turning to the cut-throat razor in my hand, and just for a moment I have doubts – just for a moment. My mind reels with the sting of the first cut, and I wince in surprise as the nerves in my wrist act to discourage my actions. But I continue to drag the razor down the length of the vein, opening a two-inch gash that seeps a surprising abundance of crimson. I watch, fascinated, my thoughts fluctuating between concerns of what – if anything – comes next, or should I rush to the bathroom and wrap my wound in a towel, quickly seeking out medical assistance? The doubts are only momentary; I think of Mehdi, and of how I have failed him, and I think of little Ayoub, and I pray this deed will not deny me reunion; then, with sodden and sticky fingers, I move the razor to my other wrist, and I open a second vein; with my legs hanging over the side of the bed, I am already beginning to feel dizzy. I welcome succumbing to the sweet release of nothing, and so I lie back and close my eyes, and the shock of the warm water swamping my face, it causes me to start.

I open confused eyes, only to find myself fully submerged beneath carmine waters, and with just one dismayed breath the bloody liquid assaults my lungs like a lance puncturing a shield;

with panicked desperation my hands reach for the sides of the stone resin bath, but sanguine fingers fail to achieve necessary purchase, and with a splash and a plop I concede to murky depths, my skull connects hard against the base of the tub, and with dizzying cognizance I note the cherry serpent spiraling from the back of my skull; I feel myself slipping deeper beneath the waters, deeper even than the depth of this tank, and I know I am sinking towards oblivion...

"What the hell?" I sit bolt upright in the bed, my body shaking and layered with rapidly cooling perspiration. I swipe the back of my hand over my face, and then run fingers through my hair, and it is no exaggeration to suggest I might have just stepped out the shower. I am sodden. The bedside clock tells me it is 3:08am. Linda lies beside me, her form reduced to little more than a silhouette in the bruising darkness, but at least the relaxed nature of her breathing indicates my outburst has eluded her; and for this I am grateful.

Pushing back the duvet I swing my legs off the mattress, and after retrieving my stick from its slot between the bedside cabinet and the bed, I move carefully through the half-light until I reach the bathroom. Only once I have closed the door do I turn on the light. I stare through a mirror darkly, at the ragged, still drenched features facing me. What did it mean? I've *traveled* many dozens of times since the accident. But I've never before experienced any sort of interaction with another person. The woman, Aya, her loss and her pain… was any of it real? And what the hell happened after that? I envisioned myself drowning, but why? And how and why did any of that link to my experience with Aya?

I wondered if perhaps any of this was connected with Mrs. Featherstone. It hadn't yet been twenty-four hours since the woman turned up looking for assistance. Had her story somehow contributed to this nightmare? I say *nightmare,* but *traveling* is a completely different experience from dreaming. So whatever had just happened, it wasn't purely fantasy.

I have so many questions, and no answers. I do know one thing though; I doubt I shall sleep again tonight. I look once again to the tired face in the mirror. The man is terribly drawn; he looks older than he did a few hours ago. I barely recognize myself, and I'm aware of something unpleasant crawling in the pit of my stomach.

Six

By the time Saturday rolled around, the concerns of my midweek nightmare had been relegated to a niggling, though still troublesome memory. I continued to run the parameters of what may have occurred, but as is the case with most things, the initial distress of the incident diminished with time.

I had risen bright and early that morning, as it was my intention to get all of my equipment packed into the Volvo, and to arrive in Claybrooke by mid-morning. I planned to spend time on Friday doing some online research into the background of the property; unfortunately, our internet service provider suffered a major glitch in their system, which meant that our house was just one of over ten thousand homes in the area to suffer a complete loss of service.

Just as I was about to set off from home, Linda came running out to the car, arms waving excitedly in the air as she called out to me, "Jack! Your mom's on the telephone. She wants to know if you are working a case.

"Crap! …What did you tell her?"

"I said she best talk to you about it."

"Good. Tell her I'm already on the road, Linz. But say I'll call her first chance I get."

"Okay. Will do." Linda didn't question my avoiding talking to Mom, although I could tell that the timing of the call troubled her. It was a bizarre situation, but one that Linda was well aware of. On three previous occasions my mother had telephoned in panic, filled with ill-feeling about a case I was working. She had, however, proven inexplicably insightful; one case in point being her forewarnings about the Dresden house, even though I had told her nothing about the investigation. It reached the stage where I actually suggested she might be psychic, but Linda laughed off this suggestion – although not very convincingly. Thenceforth, I couldn't help but wonder.

Linda clapped her hands together. "Ooh and I meant to say, the internet has started working. We're back online. Yay!"

God only knows what the neighbors must have thought. I doubt they had ever seen anyone getting quite so excited about having access to the web. Mind you, I'm not sure what they would have thought if they knew I was heading off in the hope of playing ghost buster, either. Suffice to say, we don't tend to discuss our paranormal investigations with the neighbors. They seem a strangely God-fearing bunch, and I'm guessing they would frown heavily on anything considered supernatural.

The internet connection had been reconnected far too late to allow me to research the Featherstone's cottage, but Linda (being the superstar she is), offered to spend her morning doing some research for me. She was going to check the old electoral registers; dating back as far as possible, to get a list of the property's previous occupants, just to try and clarify that Mrs. Featherstone's information regarding the previous tenants was accurate. She then intended to check for any news items online, regarding either the cottage itself or any of its past occupants.

I waved goodbye to Linda and reversed the car down the drive. The sky was pale blue, broken only by wispy strips of cotton candy, and I squinted against the glare of a lemon sun. As I reached the end of the drive I applied the brakes. Linda had skipped across the lawn and was once again standing beside the car.

I wondered if she may have changed her mind. "You've decided you're coming with…?"

"Hell no. This is your jaunt. But I will call you if I find anything interesting."

I gave it my best Humphrey Bogart impression. "Babe, you're a sweetheart."

"Wow! I never realized you did Joe Pasquale."

"Bitch."

"And don't you ever forget it."

I grinned. "How could I?"

She leaned through the open window and planted a kiss on my mouth. "Seriously, Jack. Be careful on the motorway, okay?"

I saluted her authority. "Always," I said, and then, with a toot of the horn (just to upset the neighborly God squad), I was on my way to Claybrooke.

I drove north out of town, a nest of vipers coiling in my stomach as I picked up the motorway. I hoped it was just the fact I was turning onto the M1. Since the accident, driving down that slip road is equivalent to diving off the high board. You know you can do it, and you know it'll *probably* be okay… but it's still scary shit.

It's not unheard of for me to become anxious when starting an investigation, even when it doesn't involve motorway travel. I often experience this same nervous tension, usually prior to making a first visit to the scene of an alleged happening, but I never forget that I'm lucky to be doing this sort of work. It gives me an unbelievable buzz of satisfaction each and every time I'm working a case.

I flicked on the radio as I took the short hop northwards, but reports totaling eighteen dead in Brussels, and a further thirty-five in the Paris attack, served only to pull my mind towards *that* night, and the carnage of a most grievous accident. I switched the radio off, but still it took a lot of willpower to banish dark memories from my head. This was neither the time nor place for reminiscing; certainly not about such grim matters.

Traffic was light, and in barely thirty minutes I reached the junction at Crick. From there I picked up the A5 and continued north for another thirteen miles, until I spied the slip leading onto High Cross Road. A main route leading away from the dual carriageway, cutting a swathe through labored green pastures, allowing an unhindered run towards Main Road – which feeds into the villages of Claybrooke Magna and Claybrooke Parva. The two small enclaves combined, consisted of populations numbering less than nine-hundred people. It was around this same time I realized I had left my mobile phone, and my packed lunch, at home on the kitchen table. I wasn't unduly bothered though, as I rarely have much of an appetite while I'm working. I made a mental note to call Mother once I reached home.

I turned left off Main Road into Bell St. The road was lined with a varied array of red-brick dwellings, and at its end a gated road. The gate lay open, so I continued on down the narrow lane until, and as per Mrs. Featherstone's instructions, I came upon a sharp right turn, which led down a tree-lined lane, spruces overhanging either side of the road creating a tunnel of concealment, breached only by bullets of sunlight sporadically piercing the canopy. At its deepest point, the road curved sharply upwards towards an isolated ridge some two-hundred meters in the distance. Finally, I reached the cottage just after 10:30am.

As the Volvo estate slewed to a halt on the gravel forecourt fronting the property, I admit to being somewhat surprised. Misty Ridge stood on a solitary plot. It was a picturesque little place; a red-brick, thatched cottage with slatted shutters on each window, and situated at the center of a tree lined crescent, surrounded by colorful borders of summer blooms. However, despite its initial appeal, it was quite obviously in need of external repairs. I'm no expert on such matters, but the thatch looked badly worn through. The wooden shutters were aged beyond needing a superficial coat of paint, with at least two of them splintered and hanging, and the brickwork required substantial re-pointing.

I crossed the forecourt and walked up a flower laden garden path, where I noticed large numbers of unusual looking black rocks, randomly scattered through the flower beds. The pieces varied in dimensions; ranging from rocks the size of a pea up to golf ball like chunks of metallic ore. Closer inspection confirmed my initial suspicion, the rocks were magnetite. Although I suspected their presence here proffered a mystery.

There is far more to these minerals than generally meets the eye.

My eldest sister, Helen, works as a geologist for the Frans Bien Institute, and she had once gifted me a lodestone the size of a sprout. I pulled my car keys from my pocket, testing them against several of the pieces. I was right. None of the scattered rocks I tested was regular magnetite; the soil appeared layered with magnetized lodestones, though even stranger was the fact there appeared to be bedrock of slate beneath the topsoil.

This is weird.

Not only was it strange to find pieces such as these in such abundance, but also because of the ground in which they lay. Slate bedrock is not a place to find such stones; they usually exist in sandy deposits. I made a mental note to mention this oddity to my sister, when next we exchanged emails, and then proceeded on towards the somewhat out of kilter with the rest of the property, but nevertheless impressive looking front door, adorned with intricately carved roses cut into each of its panels. I rang the bell and waited, patiently. After a few minutes I rang it again. I waited several minutes before ringing the bell for a third – and final – time. Still getting no reply, I raised my fist with the intention of giving the door a hefty knock. Before my hand could strike, the door was flung open and I was greeted by a tall, wiry man with sun bronzed skin and the features of a meerkat. He held a child in his arms.

"Sorry about that," he apologized. "I did hear the bell, but I was upstairs dressing the little man, here." He gestured with his head towards the boy.

"Not a problem," I replied. "I'm Jack. Jack Keswick."

"Yes?"

It was obvious from the blank expression on his face, that my name meant absolutely nothing to the man.

"You know," I pressed, "I'm from Keswick Investigations? Your wife asked me to call. I'm a paranormal investigator. I take it that you are Mark?"

A look of realization dawned on the man's face.

"It's Marcus actually. But, oh god, of course, I'm sorry. We have been talking for weeks about getting someone in to try and sort this out. I didn't realize the missus had actually arranged for you to call, though."

"She didn't tell you?" I queried.

"No, but to be honest, Jack, we're not exactly getting on all that great at the moment. I've been working the night shift for the last two weeks. Needless to say, my leaving her and the little man alone at night; especially with all of the weird stuff going on in this place; well, let's just say that it hasn't made me very popular."

I nodded sympathetically. "Well then, let's hope I can help put this problem to rest then."

Taking a step back from the doorway, Marcus invited me into their home, urging that I watch my step as I crossed the raised threshold. It is not uncommon for people to concern themselves once they realize my ungainly stride, but I still prefer to think myself more capable than most give credit. Still, his words were warm and spoken with good intention.

I followed him through into a compact lounge which smelled heavily of stale cigarette smoke, and, upon invitation; I took a seat on the sofa.

Marcus informed me his wife had nipped out to pick up some household supplies from a shop in the next village, but that she should be back within twenty minutes at most. I told him this wasn't a problem as I actually wanted to carry out a short interview with him, just to get his personal take on the events which had been occurring. Placing his son down onto a play mat on the floor, Marcus said he would stick the kettle on and make us a brew.

As he left the room, I became aware of the air temperature dipping a couple of degrees, and the child, who had been happily banging together a couple of wooden play bricks, suddenly started to cry. I wasn't sure whether this was just a case of the youngster becoming upset because he had now been denied the comfort zone of both parents. Or, just maybe, he had an inkling of some other presence, and it was this causing his upset. If nothing else, these investigations have led me to believe that children have an awareness that extends way beyond that of most adults.

I spoke to the boy, smiling as I did so. My words seemed to soothe him, and so, using my cane for support, I allowed myself to slip to a sitting position on the floor beside him. Then I attempted to build a tower of bricks. Every time it reached four stacks high, the youngster took great delight in smashing the tower down. I pretended to be upset with the destruction of my handiwork, and rubbed my eyes, tearfully, and this had the boy laughing uncontrollably. By the time Marcus returned from the kitchen with two mugs of steaming hot tea, his son was sitting happily on the play mat, beside me, still gleefully rejoicing at my mock despair.

Marcus placed both of the steaming refreshments down on top of the dining table, set a safe distance away from where his son was playing.

"Help yourself when you're ready," he offered, gesturing towards the drinks, "but you may want to give it a minute. It'll need to cool a bit."

I thanked him.

"So," asked Marcus, sitting himself down on the sofa, "how exactly does this work?"

My joints ached as I climbed up off the floor, and Marcus was good enough to take my arm and give me a hoist-up.

"Thanks," I said. As I returned to the sofa there was a loud clicking sound from somewhere along my spine.

"Jesus!" Marcus said, startled. "What the hell was that?"

"It's okay," I said. "It's a long story, but the short version is, I was involved in a serious accident a few years ago. I've got quite a bit of titanium holding me together, and sometimes sitting in one position for too long… well, things tend to set."

"Ouch, sounds nasty," Marcus sympathized. He gestured towards my leg, "Is that how you got the…?"

"Yes," I said. "But it's fine, honestly…and to answer your question about how this works. Well, I already have your wife's version of events. I'd like to take a few minutes now, to try and get you to tell me exactly what's been going on, from your own viewpoint, you understand? Then, perhaps, you might show me around the property. You know, point out the places there have been hotspots of activity, if that's okay?"

"Yes, of course. Well, I don't quite know how to begin really."

"Just start at the beginning, Marcus," I flicked the record button on my Dictaphone. "You don't mind if I take notes?"

"No, that's fine. Well, things were great when we first got this place. It was special. Our own *first home* or at least the first one we actually owned. We had the apartment in Leicester, but it doesn't really feel like home when you are paying rent on it, you know? We took this place on knowing it needed plenty of work, but that was a part of the appeal really. We had a chance to put our own stamp on the place, turn it into the type of family home that we always wanted…" I could see his mind beginning to drift to another time and place.

"Please, go on," I urged, not wanting his thoughts to lose traction.

He took a resolute sigh, and seemed to melt into the sofa. "I was at work when it first started. When I got home I found the missus in a right state. She reckoned there had been people in the house, talking, and then shouting at each other."

"Any sign of a break-in?" I had to ask, although I already knew what his answer would be.

Marcus shook his head. "No, nothing like that. And, to be honest with you, back then I was worried about my wife. She only ever seemed to hear the voices when I was at work. It was always when she and the little man were here by themselves. Honestly, at first I began to suspect she was on the verge of a breakdown."

"But you don't think that now?" I queried.

"No, I don't. Not now. She had been telling me about the voices for maybe a fortnight or more... and then I heard them too.

"My wife was upstairs in the bath. I was downstairs, feeding the little man. Suddenly, I noticed the temperature in the room had cooled... and when I say cooled, I mean dramatically. The next thing I knew was the sound of a full blown row going on upstairs in our bedroom. Two voices, a male and a female arguing violently. I rushed upstairs expecting to find my wife confronting an intruder, but instead I found her cowering in the bath. The raised voices continued all around us, and then these were added to by the sound of a young child crying.

"Since that night, things have gotten steadily worse; furniture rearranges itself, lights and taps turn themselves on and off on a daily basis. We have had the place rewired and all of the plumbing checked, but to no avail. It's a nightmare really, and from a financial point of view we are stuck here. Although, if I'm being completely honest, neither of us wants to spend any more time under this roof than we have to."

We sat in silence for a few moments after Marcus finished speaking. I could tell from the tone in his voice, this was a man under immense emotional stress. However, as excited as I personally was about the prospects this case presented, I didn't want to alienate my host by seeming to rush him in his recollection of these paranormal events. Finally, though, I spoke.

"So, tell me, Marcus, what areas of the cottage would you class as hot-spots for activity?"

Placing his head in the cupped bowl of his hands, he sat silently, as if praying for some unknown deity to relieve the weight of his burden. After a period of uneasy quiet, and without any warning, he suddenly stiffened his shoulders and turned to face me. "Did she tell you? Did she tell you everything?"

"Why don't you tell me, Marcus? Tell me in your own words," I said, somewhat bemused by the way he had emphasized *everything*."

"It always starts upstairs," he said. "Sure, the furniture and other stuff gets moved all over the place, but the voices always start upstairs. The flashing lights always start upstairs. And it's always the taps in the bathroom that get turned on and off –"

"Go on," I urged.

"Did she tell you?" he repeated, with a level of concern new to our conversation.

I shook my head. "I don't think she told me about whatever it is bothering you. Perhaps you need to –"

"Okay," he answered brusquely. "I'm sorry," he said. "I don't mean to snap. It's just… worrying, and a little embarrassing."

"Please," I said, "whatever it is, it may help talking to a stranger."

He nodded. "Last week, while the missus nipped over to the next village to pick up some diapers, I intended on making a start renewing some of the shutters. I don't know if you noticed, but some of the wood around those windows is rotten."

"Okay," I said.

"She reckons she was out for barely fifteen minutes. Returning home, she found me sitting in a hot bath."

"You changed your mind about the repairs?"

"You don't understand. I was sitting in a steaming hot bath, clutching a razor to my wrist. To all intent and purposes I was in a fugue state."

The words hit like a sledgehammer to my head. I felt sickly dizzy. Had my dream been some sort of clairvoyant flash, or was it merely coincidence? Leaving my body, or *traveling* to use a term I prefer, has been a regular – though still untamed – ability since the accident. It is not something I can do at will, but it does happen. However, I have never personally demonstrated any other sorts of psychic ability. So why would I now?

"How did your wife react, when she found you like that?"

Marcus smirked uncomfortably. "Wow, I guess she really didn't give you the full skinny."

"What do you mean?"

"Of course it distressed her, but I doubt it came as too big a shock."

"And why is that?" I asked.

"Because it was the fifth time in six weeks that she had found me sitting in a bath holding a razor to my wrists."

My mouth fell open – the dream could not have been coincidence. "Jesus," I whispered.

"I doubt if Jesus has any intention of helping me," Marcus said. "Doctors can't help me either. I've had a brain scan, and all sorts of other tests." He shook his head, "Nothing at all wrong with me. Clean bill of health, at least physically. I'm booked to see a shrink on Tuesday, need to talk about my suicidal tendencies." Marcus snorted. "I've never been suicidal. And yet," he gestured towards the child, "Until I get my mental health sorted, the quacks are recommending I'm not left in sole charge of the little man."

I looked at him from beneath raised brows. "Yet your wife still trusts you enough to leave him in your care?"

Marcus sat forward in his seat, arms wide and palms facing up as he looked me in the eye. "This is the thing; you see we've worked out that it doesn't happen while the little fella is here."

"Really?" I said. "Could that not be a coincidence, the timing I mean?"

"I guess so. But the simple fact is that I only lose time and act like I'm out to top myself, when I'm alone in the house."

"Christ," I said, and for the first time I regretted Violet's absence. I had a sickening fear that I may be into something way above my pay grade.

Marcus passed his son a beaker of juice, and then he retrieved our teas from the table. He handed me the still warm mug. "Jack, I apologize, because I know I probably seem a bit off, but it's only because we are at breaking point. Trust me, I am grateful my wife contacted you, and I'm elated you are here. So, please, tell me, what do you think any of this means?"

"It means," I said, rising achingly to my feet, and regretting my earlier decision to join the infant on the floor, "that we have located the source area for the events that are transpiring. And this gives us a very good place to start."

Seven

I explained to Marcus that whenever a haunting occurs, regardless of whether it is a ghost or a spirit which is making itself known, there is always a focal point, or hotspot of energy. Locating that area goes a long way towards resolving the visitations.

I suggested that, rather than him showing me around the upstairs area of the property; it might be a good idea for me to have a look around by myself. This way I might get a better sense of anything relating to a presence within the home. Marcus seemed more than happy to agree to this. In fact, I got the distinct impression he was daunted by the prospect of seeking out whatever was haunting the cottage.

I swallowed down the dregs of my tea and handed the mug to Marcus. Then I made my way upstairs. Gripping the wooden banister with one hand and holding my cane in the other, as I struggled with climbing the steep and narrow staircase. I was aware of Marcus standing at the bottom of the stairs, clutching his small son in his arms. I could almost feel the man's eyes burning into the back of my head, and I couldn't help but wonder exactly what it must have been like for Marcus and his wife. To find them stuck in such a place, plagued with the sort of activity present here, it hardly bears thinking about.

Reaching the top of the stairs I turned right and walked along the landing, noting a drop in temperature as I did so. The only source of illumination was through a small paned window, and this allowed a narrow bleed of sunlight to mark my path, but the landing remained cooler than seemed reasonable. Upon entering the door at the far end of the corridor, I found myself in the property's bathroom; as dark as the landing had been, it appeared to be in mid-restoration. In the centre of the room there stood a white stone resin bath, which as best I could recall seemed identical to the one in which I almost drowned. I couldn't help but stand and stare at this beautifully symmetrical object, and I wondered how something so uniform could instill such unease in my heart. The tub was raised on legs of decorative brass; the taps on the bath were also ornamental, as were the ones on the fancy hand basin fitted at the far wall, beneath a frosted glass window that restricted the light in the room to a dull and dirty gray. A gleaming white toilet, set against the wall to the left of me, completed the suite.

These items all looked expensive. However, bathroom walls that were in obvious need of re-plastering, and the scuffed, bare floorboards, pointed to the fact that this part of the cottage was still a work in progress. My jaw clenched as something sizeable scurried in the cavity wall. Mice rather than rats, I hoped. I wondered if the Featherstones owned a cat. I'd certainly seen no sign of one.

It occurred to me that this room, in fact the whole upstairs of the property, was laden with a heavy atmosphere. It was as though it carried a burden, something ponderous, which waited in solemn silence for the day of its revelation.

My musings were interrupted by the sound of a car beeping its horn, as it pulled up onto the hard-standing at the front of the property. The sound of Marcus opening the front door and engaging in conversation with a female voice, confirmed for me my cardinal impression that his wife had returned home from her shopping trip. I listened, and although I couldn't actually make out their words, it was obvious from the tone of their voices that the initial warmth of the greeting between them had quickly cooled to a more fraught level of communication. I remembered what both Marcus and his wife had told me, about how the goings on in their home were placing a tremendous strain on their relationship.

I decided that, rather than going downstairs in the hope my presence would somehow placate the couple's disagreement, it would be for the best if I were to just carry on with my investigation of Misty Ridge.

Walking back along the landing, I opened a couple of doors; one of which housed the boiler, and another which served as a broom cupboard. I made my way towards the two remaining doors, both of which were at the other end of the corridor.

As I opened the first of these, I was greeted with the prettiest sight I had seen in the cottage so far. Little Jacob's bedroom walls had been painted lemon, and this set off wonderfully against the pastel blue carpet and curtains. The boy's cot sat in one corner of the room, alongside a matching wardrobe and a set of drawers. On the walls were prints of various cartoon characters. I couldn't help but smile as the scene before me stirred memories of the plans Linda and I had made, though which fate ultimately saw fit to deny. Mine was a smile soon faded; reality biting hard.

I realized that the sound of raised voices downstairs had abated, and this provided a measure of relief. I had no desire to be central to a domestic spat.

As I moved back out onto the landing, I was vaguely aware of another vehicle arriving at the cottage; its tires screeching as it pulled to a halt on the gravel outside. All thoughts of who it may have been disappeared as Mrs. Featherstone appeared at the top of the stairs. My mind had been elsewhere as the woman stepped off the staircase and onto the landing before me, giving me something of a start. She was clutching the now sleeping child against her chest, and I assumed she intended on putting Jacob down for a nap.

"Hello, Jack." The wry smile creasing her lips was, I believe, more to do with the look of surprise on my face, rather than being especially pleased to see me. "Sorry if I made you jump."

"It's ok," I replied, smiling; in a vain attempt not to look a complete imbecile. "Not a good idea to sneak up on people though, especially in a haunted house."

She smiled again, this time it was more forced though. "Did you hear?" she asked, gesturing downstairs with her hand.

I nodded. "Yes, I heard the argument, but I couldn't hear what was being said – just raised voices," I said, doing my utmost to emphasize I hadn't pried into her marital strife.

Edging past me, she opened the door which led into the main bedroom. "I'm sorry, Jack, I know that you have work you want to do, but all of this is really getting to me. I think I need to go lie down for a little while. I hope you don't mind?"

I did mind. I had traveled a distance to try and help this family sort out their ethereal goings on, and to do this I would need full access to the property and its occupants. Having said that, the woman looked even more drained of energy than when we had first met. Her skin was dull. Her hair lifeless and the circles under her eyes deep black saucers. "It's okay." I said, nodding reassuringly. "You take some time. Have a little rest. I'll give the rest of the place a once over."

"Thank you, Jack," she sighed, taking my hand in hers, and giving it a gentle squeeze.

I shuddered slightly at the coolness of her skin. It was obvious to me that the woman wasn't quite right. Perhaps she was anemic or suffered from poor circulation. Either way, her husband should insist she visit the doctor and get a full check-up.

She was just about to close the bedroom door, when she stopped and raised her forefinger in the air. "Listen," she said, straining her ears. "Do you hear that? I think it's starting again…"

She was right. Raised voices were coming from downstairs – male and female voices. My first thought was that people in the house were arguing, but then I remembered what both Marcus and Sally had said: It often sounded like this, but upon investigation there was never anyone to be found.

I turned and headed downstairs just as fast as my gimp leg would carry me. Upon reaching the bottom step I was greeted by a surreal sight. Midway between the open front door and the position where I now stood, two blondes were involved in a heated exchange. The woman farthest from me wore comfortable house clothes – a purple t-shirt and a pair of white sweats. She was agitatedly waving a folder in the face of the other woman; a thick-set lady, bronzed to the point of being orange, and dressed in a casual blouse and slacks. Marcus, who was attempting to place himself between the two, had his open hands raised before him, his palms facing outwards in what appeared to be a gesture aimed at calming the situation.

For a moment I stood watching in silence, considering whether I had any business becoming embroiled in whatever was going on. I hadn't reached a decision when my jaw dropped open.

The white shirted blonde with her back to me turned slightly, which meant I could now see clearly the face of the antagonist with the folder. It was Linda.

"Linz?" My sudden call brought their verbal battle to an abrupt end. The trio turned in unison to face me. "What the hell is going on? What are you doing here?" At this point I was completely dumbfounded. I had left my wife back in Northampton. She had no business being here.

"And who the hell is this?" yelled the woman, who, due to a skin tone of flight-attendant orange, and features not dissimilar to a used teabag, I immediately surmised had a propensity for sunbeds and cigarettes.

"Like I tried to tell you," snapped Linda. "This is my husband, and I really need to speak with him."

"You didn't try to tell me anything," replied the woman, her tone moderately calmer, although still irate. "You just screeched at me that you had to come into my house. Marcus, what the bloody hell is going on here?"

Marcus looked as perplexed as I felt.

"What are you talking about, Faye? This is Jack Keswick. You know; the paranormal investigator."

"How would I know that?" disputed the woman whom Marcus had referred to as Faye.

"Just a minute," I interrupted. "Firstly, if you don't mind my asking, who are you? And secondly, Linz, what's happened? Why are you here?"

Linda opened her mouth to speak, but before she got the chance to reply to my questions, the tangerine-blonde beat her to it.

"Who am I? I'm Faye Staunton, and this is our crappy, bloody, horrible house you are in! So, who sodding well told *you* about it?"

I turned to Marcus. "I don't understand."

"Neither do I, mate," he replied, perplexed. "You told me that you had met Faye."

"What? Faye is your wife? But that doesn't…?"

Linda chose this moment to flip open the folder she was holding. I saw that it contained a number of A4 sized sheets of paper, upon which were printed photocopies of various articles, which I assumed my wife had downloaded from the internet.

"It's what I've been trying to say, Jack. I tried to call you, but then I realized you had left home without your phone. So I drove out here –" I didn't need to wait for her to finish.

I had barely taken a moment to read any of the headlines on the articles my wife held copies of. All that my eyes registered was one photo. This had been enough. I turned around and even though my back, legs and side were aching, I made it halfway up the staircase before Linda completed her sentence.

As I struggled onto the landing, I heard the first screams emanating from the main bedroom. I became aware of an acrid smell and the taint of smoke began to smart my eyes; behind me I could hear Linda, Marcus and his wife, as they too hurried up the stairs.

I could feel heat radiating through the door even before I reached the end of the landing, and yet, without time for rational thought, I turned the handle and entered the room. The sight that greeted me was something that will haunt until my dying day. Mrs. Featherstone was kneeling in the centre of the double bed, screaming as flames surrounded her. The fire belched up from the mattress with harsh intent, brushing her body with glowing licks of pain. Only then did I realize that in her arms she still held Jacob. The infant squealed a terrible cry, and she held him with such vigor that I half suspected he might "pop" like a squeezed balloon. The mother's arms could offer nothing save a vain attempt at protection for her son, and she too uttered a cacophony of high pitched howls; her form wracked by the searing blaze. The fire reached past the woman's torso, and even above her screams I realized I was listening to the infant's death cry. The flames clawed at her head, her hair turning to a web of black tar that crawled across her skull, shrinking in reluctance at the fiery onslaught. I watched horrified as orange flames danced about the bed, and I realized there was little hope. Both mother and child were a simmering lost cause, but still, without sensible thought for my own wellbeing, I lunged towards the bed and, for the briefest moment, was able to grab hold of the blazing woman. It was a vain effort. I attempted to pull her clear of the inferno, but the fire forced me to release my grip. The intense heat scorched against my face, and then, suddenly, and without any logical reason, it felt as though I was being yanked backwards. As I tumbled clear of the flames, my head crashing first against the wall and then downwards, hard onto the floor, stinging tears burned my eyeballs. A stink of unattended char grill filling my nostrils.

Linda and Faye had been screaming since arriving on the landing, but as I fell I noticed my wife's eyes on me. She looked horrified.

Quickly I realized why.

The flesh of my right arm had been burned away; eaten down to the very bone. Only a stinking, greasy-black stump remained, smoldering with putrid remnants of what had once been a limb.

To be honest, there was surprisingly little pain. I realized the nerve endings in my arm had been eaten away in the inferno. But still I screamed.

Marcus tore a flannel dressing gown from a hook on the back of the door. He began valiantly attempting to beat down the flames enveloping the bed. In this at least, he seemed to be having some success. Although he let out howls of agony each time the flames whipped at his arms. In the end though, his efforts proved to be of no real avail.

Both mother and child remained in that same upright position. Two bodies, melded into one grotesque caricature of something that had once been life. Mrs. Featherstone's head was a black blister, stained with swollen boils of orange-yellow glow. She had ceased to be a woman, and now served only as the ruined wick of a monumental candle. I lay back on the floor and closed my eyes, knowing, as consciousness fell away from me, that I had failed in my mission to save them.

Eight

Rain thuds against the windscreen like the beats of an insane drummer. I struggle even with seeing past the hood of the car. My wiper blades are swishing like amphetamine powered metronomes, but still vision remains negligible as bullets of water pelt the vehicle. Twenty minutes ago this had been just another gray late-November afternoon. Then the monsoon appeared, almost without warning, and this side of the motorway became a landing strip of lights as drivers reacted by reducing speed in accordance with the conditions. The inclement weather forced the majority to drop to below forty, although, as is always the case, some morons still appeared intent on risking life and limb with driving more inclined to the racetrack.

It is one of those rare days when conditions are so bad I actually fear continuing on. The poor visibility is made worse by the water distorted flash of headlights on the opposite side of the road, and every now and again I am forced to dip my head as the blinding beams of a lorry stings my vision. A number of drivers have already taken the decision to pull up on the hard shoulder. Others have ground to a halt on the inside lane, and although I can understand their reasoning behind coming to a stop while still on the motorway, I can only imagine things ending badly, probably with some poor sap losing their life in a catastrophic rear-shunting. If I was on any minor road, then doubtless I too would make the same decision and pull over to wait out the storm. However, setting aside just how stressful this journey has become, I am only eighteen miles south of Northampton. If I continue on, even at this speed I should be home inside of forty-five minutes.

It seems almost impossible, but the rain appears to be falling even harder and faster now. I squeeze the steering wheel, as though holding it firmly will somehow guarantee me continued safe passage. My speed is reduced to barely more than twenty, and it is with owl-wide eyes I struggle to make out the road laid before me. I concentrate on Linda, knowing that if this weather has reached Northampton, she will be growing concerned for my safety. A thought flashes through my mind that I really ought to pull over. My wipers are operating at full-pelt and still I can barely see in front of the car. I consider pulling up directly onto the verge beyond the hard shoulder. The problem I have is that I can no longer see the inside lane, let alone the hard shoulder. So no, I have little option other than to stay in this lane and continue on. I can only pray the fates will be kind.

But the Moirai are never kind.

I am blinded by the sudden glare of headlights in the corner of my eye, and in that moment I fail to understand the odd angle of the beam, nor why it appears to be directly approaching me. The truck careers through the central reservation barrier, approaching my vehicle as though from a two-o'clock position. The big wagon hits me virtually side on, its right headlight a searchlight of doom as it connects with the driver side door; later they will pull shards of broken lantern from my damaged body, but for now the jarring shock of the impact numbs any pain.

As the truck continues snaking across the three lanes – its trailer lashing two more vehicles and the roadside barrier before finally conceding to the incline of the embankment – my Golf is shunted sideways, and as the vehicle flips into a roll that will carry me off-road, I think only of how much I will miss Linda, and the hurt my demise will cause her. Tumbling through the air, time slowing almost to a stop, it is through a rotating blur of dizzying concussion that I note the approaching crash barrier, and in this instant I wonder if it is sturdy enough to bring my nightmare to a halt; and, if so, might it not yet prove my savior?

The barricade achieves its purpose, but still, the impact of the Golf's roll and accelerated skid along the length of the barrier distorts its frame, twisting and fragmenting the integrity of the structure, until finally it tears itself apart; the ruptured steel beam skewers the onrushing Golf, punching a fissure through the engine block of the vehicle, and on; until kinetic motion draws the girder past the steering column, a lance into my chest.

I lose consciousness, although perhaps only momentarily, and then I open my eyes to a realization the limb of steel has passed through me, penetrating my right side and exiting out the back of the seat in which I am trapped. Amid my confusion, I tell myself everything is going to be alright. It hurts when I breathe. It hurts really badly; but I remain conscious; despite the pain, I realize this must be a good thing. My groin feels wet, and I wonder if I've pissed myself. And then I note the blood draining from my gored chest, and I understand this giant splinter will end me. I close my eyes and picture Linda's beautiful smile, and I would give anything just to hold her in my arms.

I observe the proceedings with fascinated interest, giving no thought to the fact that, inexplicably, I am somehow looking down from on high at the rescue crews working tirelessly. Like a systematically precise machine, one team of firemen is tearing open the hood, then cutting wires to remove the battery; another crew use more elaborate gear to shear what remains of the roof from the flattened vehicle. Only once these tasks are completed, then will they be in a position to rescue, or perhaps simply recover the body of the poor soul trapped within. From my bird's-eye vantage, I look up and down the stretch of road.

Perhaps bizarrely, the storm chooses this moment to abate, no doubt content with the carnage it has worked. The Golf was not the big wagon's only victim. Before crossing the central reservation barrier, the truck wiped out two vehicles on the northbound carriage. From my viewpoint it is impossible to identify the make or purpose of either automobile, surrounded as they are by rescue vehicles, and a bustling plethora of bodies. On this side of the carriageway there is far greater ruination, though less need for haste from those assisting. The truck has come to a stop on the embankment; a number of vehicles park close by, but other than the beacons identifying their purpose, their occupants seem to delay taking immediate action. I understand the driver is already lost; his heart having given out prior to the accident, and although I cannot explain the 'how' of my knowing, I do understand this. The heavy-load wagon poses no further threat, its front end twisted awry on the incline; the flipped trailer lying almost ninety degrees to the cab. Away to my right, an upended Mercedes has pancaked on its roof, broken like a dropped omelet; neither the thirty-year old mother nor either of her two daughters will see another morning. A hundred meters along the carriageway, still more flashing lights, still more carnage. The boy, who minutes ago was driving the Corsa, just days ago celebrated his nineteenth birthday; he will not see his twentieth. It is a panorama of destruction, devastation and death, and yet I remain serene.

I understand now.

There is a far greater purpose. Reality exists as a tidal sphere and all of this is just an experience. Existence played out amid a swirling ocean of possibilities. We are all 'just an experience'. The snake of time doesn't chase its tail, but reality is a circumference without beginning or end.

Below me fire crews exchange position with paramedics, and it now becomes their turn to busy themselves working on the figure trapped in the Golf. As one set of rescuers prepare cutting gear capable of burning through the length of steel pinning the man's chest, others work hard to sustain him. I am fascinated by their coordination.

Neither wind nor rain returns. And although an abundance of flashing lights continues to act as the marker to this catastrophe, in truth they have no impact upon the tranquility behind my eyes.

When, finally, they succeed in freeing the pale figure, a meter length shard of steel still pricking his chest, it occurs to me just how much of a resemblance we share, he and I. Then a thought creeps into me, and for the first time I start to experience something akin to disquiet. I am not afraid, but the thought I may be removed from this quietude, only then to be stuffed back inside that damaged meat sack. The contemplation causes my shoulders to cramp; I suffer the disappointment of a child at the funfair, riding his favorite attraction and knowing that in moments the ride will end, and then it will be time to return home.

Below me, the perforated man is placed onto a stretcher and carried towards an ambulance. Some of the firemen begin whooping and exchanging high-fives. Even as I consider these oddly inappropriate actions, a tickle of spider webs moves over my face and down my body. Something begins tugging on my form, gently at first like a light summer breeze, though quickly it builds to a momentum irresistible, pulling me away from the overhead where I currently reside, back towards that place where I now know we exist as but a fraction of our potential...

Nine

Consciousness returned through a billowing haze, and I found myself struggling to focus on those loitering over me, their bone-white features shifting amid a fog of confusion, worried faces emerging, appearing like a trio of moons simultaneously breaking through dense cloud.

They tell me I have been unconscious for almost five minutes. It feels as though I have been out for hours. At first I wonder why these people are leaning over my prone body, fussing about my wellbeing. Then I remember what has happened; I think about the mother and her child, and of my fire ravaged arm, and my body begins to quiver as the tears overcome me.

Even as I struggle to sit up, I continue to wail at the returning memories. Linda flings herself around me, and hugs me gently.

Over and again she keeps repeating the same phrase: "It's okay. It's okay. It's okay." Despite her assurances, and as much as it shames me to say it, I continue bawling like a chastised child.

Finally, Marcus, who had initially been standing behind me, interceded. Moving to take hold of my shoulders then looking me straight in the eye, he insisted, "Mr. Keswick, stop it. Stop it now, Jack. You're okay. Look at your arm. Look at your arm, man!"

His pleas succeeded in restoring some modicum of sanity, and between stuttering sobs my composure began to return. Until, finally, I was able to stop shaking.

It wasn't until this point that I realized just what it was they were trying to make me understand. I stared in disbelief through tear stained eyes at my arm. I opened and closed my right hand, stretching out my fingers then closing them into a tight fist. I watched fascinated as muscles and veins moved beneath the taut flesh of my hand and arm. I stared at the love heart tattoo on the back of my right forearm, and the scroll beneath it declaring *Jack Loves Linda, Forever.* Linda and I had only been together six weeks when, after a few too many beers, I decided on getting some body art. The tattoo had been written off as craziness by everyone who knew me. But I never once regretted getting it. I knew, even back then, she was the only girl for me.

So there I was, sitting on the floor in the home of two people who were all but strangers to me, staring with a mix of awe and elated relief at the sight of my outstretched arm; a limb which moments earlier had been burned to a ruined stump.

"I don't understand? It doesn't make any sense?" I challenged, hoping that some inexplicable burst of inspiration would help rationalize what had happened to me.

It was Faye who spoke first, and as she did so, I couldn't help but stare at the smoky tracks staining her amber cheeks.

"I think it does make sense, Jack. I think that your wife has worked it out. She showed us the folder."

"Oh God," I said, my mind suddenly recalling the full horror of the situation. "The woman and the child, they were both on the bed when it went up."

"Jack, please, you need to try and remain calm," urged Linda, soothing the backs of her fingers against my cheek. "It's okay, honey. Just look at the bed. It's okay."

"What –?" I never finished the sentence. My eyes turned towards the pine bed, the matching pillowcases and duvet cover, each patterned with bright summer flowers against a cream colored backdrop, which made up the bedding set. Neither bed, nor bedding, showed any sign of damage. Only then did I realize the room no longer carried the acrid taint of smoke, neither was the aroma of burned flesh palpable in the air. "I just don't understand." I whispered. "It did happen, didn't it?"

"Yes, Jack," Linda replied. "We all saw it. It really did happen."

"Here," urged Marcus, handing me the yellow folder with which Linda had arrived at the house. "I think you should take a look at this. It may explain an awful lot about what has been going on."

"You saved me, Marcus. It was you pulled me clear of the fire."

A doubtful expression painted his features. "It wasn't. And I didn't."

"I felt your hands on my shoulders."

"No. I think it was a burst of heat threw you backwards, lifted you clean off your feet.

I stared at him. His assessment made little sense, but he had no answers for me. Any further protestations would be pointless.

"Why don't we go downstairs?" proposed Faye, who looked as decidedly unsettled by the whole affair as I was feeling. "Then I can make us all a coffee…or perhaps something stronger. I think we all agree that Jack needs to read what's in that folder."

"Good idea," echoed Linda, handing me the cane she had retrieved from the floor. Her eyes declaring she was ready to vacate the scene of what had been a most horrendous event.

As we left the room I cast a look back in the direction of the bed. I needed to confirm for my own peace of mind that, whatever we had witnessed, it had taken place on some other level of reality. Somehow, although we all watched the horror unfold, we hadn't *really* witnessed a woman and her child burning to death. I breathed a huge sigh of relief at the sight of the Staunton's bed standing as it was, undamaged in the center of the room. Then, I turned and followed the others along the landing and down the narrow staircase. The icy water running along my veins served to hasten my gait.

Once we reached the lounge, I slumped in a high-backed chair. The two women occupied the sofa directly opposite me, while Marcus opted to remain standing. I could feel their eyes on me as I stared long and hard at the folder resting in my lap. Marcus had scooped up his now sleeping son from the play mat, cradling him in a manner which suggested the father was gleaning much needed comfort from this close contact. The sleeping boy remained thankfully oblivious to the horrors that had occurred upstairs. The child – who only now did I discover was named Peter – had managed to sleep through the entire argument between Linda and his mother, and also those other terrible events.

He was a lucky boy.

The two women disappeared into the kitchen, and I heard the sound of a kettle being filled.

I became aware of Marcus edging his way towards the door. I got the distinct impression he would have preferred to join his spouse in the kitchen, but instead felt obliged to stay with me. I guess he understood my need for moral support, and likely he desired the same of his wife. He stood for a few moments shuffling uncomfortably by the door, and then he cleared his throat and said my name, before excusing himself under pretense of helping with the drinks.

I waved him away: "Sure, no problem." And then I was alone. I sat for a few more minutes; silently staring at the folder in my lap, until eventually I plucked up courage to open it.

There were numerous articles Linda had downloaded; although a majority was census lists and electoral registers. However, one particular copy of a newspaper clipping chilled my bones, as did the photo accompanying the story. I sat transfixed, staring at a studio portrait of Mrs. Featherstone and her husband Mark, cradling their young son. As I read the banner headline my head began to swim, and for a moment I had to battle to stop myself fainting.

The Leicester Clarion - Monday, March 16th, 1987

Horror discovery for father as flames claim family

TRAGEDY struck at the weekend in the sleepy village of Claybrooke. Mark Featherstone returned to his two-hundred-year-old cottage, after finishing work at 8:30am on Friday, March 13th, to find his wife Sally, 25, and 18 month old son Jacob, in the main bedroom, dead – ravaged by fire; fire investigators have yet to confirm the cause of the blaze, although it is believed that a faulty electric blanket may have contributed to the untimely deaths.

The sight which greeted Mr. Featherstone, upon his return from work, was one the horror of which is hard to imagine. All was quiet within the quaint cottage, which Mr. Featherstone shared with his young family, and he had assumed his wife and child were still sleeping. Although he became aware of what he would later describe as *'a faint but sickly-sweet smell in the air.'*

Nevertheless, he had decided to cook himself breakfast and take a shower, before disturbing his family from their slumber.

It was approximately 9.40am when Mr. Featherstone made his gruesome discovery. Having finished showering, he entered his son's bedroom to check on the child. He found his son's cot to be empty, but this did not unduly worry the father as the boy often woke during the night and ended up sleeping in his parents' bed. However, it was upon entering the main bedroom of their home that Mr. Featherstone discovered the true horror of what had occurred. The still smoldering bodies of his wife and child were lying on the bed; their bones fused together by the incredible heat which had been generated by the flames which engulfed them. Incredibly, there was virtually no fire damage to the rest of the property, other than to the mattress and the frame of the bed itself. With early reports having suggested that there was no obvious cause for the fire, some media outlets are identifying it as a possible case of (S.H.C.) *spontaneous human combustion,* a suggestion which is being strongly rebuked by members of both the police and fire services.

Last night the property was visited by Professor Stephen Ranking, head of the Leicestershire Police Forensic Science Department. Professor Rankin, whilst speaking exclusively to this newspaper, has confirmed that he believes the alleged spontaneous combustion theory can be readily explained away by a number of interconnecting but nonetheless tragic circumstances.

Mark Featherstone has, according to Professor Ranking, confirmed that his wife was nervous about being left alone in the house at nights while he was working. Mrs. Featherstone would regularly have a glass of brandy before going to bed, as she claimed it helped her to sleep. It is believed Sally Featherstone had also recently visited her General Practitioner, and that he had prescribed her a course of sleeping tablets. Tragically, it would appear Mrs. Featherstone had taken more than the prescribed dosage of her medication. This may have been an accident on her part, as early post mortem results also suggest she drank up to five units of alcohol on the night she died. All of which contributed to the fact that, when the fire broke out, Mrs. Featherstone probably didn't wake up; at least until it was far too late for her and the child.

Professor Ranking stated that Geoff Chown, of the Leicestershire Fire Service, had confirmed to him that the cause of the fire was actually a wiring fault in the electric blanket Mrs. Featherstone had been using to heat her bed. The Professor believes that the copious amount of alcohol the deceased woman had consumed, contributed to what he referred to as *the wick effect.*

The Professor stated: "This whole case is an absolute tragedy. This fire, which started due to an electrical fault, would normally have burnt itself out in a relatively short space of time; due to its point of origin being in a small, and reasonably contained room. Once the oxygen in the room had exhausted itself, the fire should have been extinguished. However, the alcohol in Mrs. Featherstone's body, combined with both her and her child's body fat, created what I can best describe as *a human candle*. If you can imagine a candle which has been reversed, so that the wax is on the inside and the wick is on the outside, this is what has occurred here. The woman's night clothes and the bedding itself have acted like a burning wick. Meanwhile, the alcohol, when combined with the fats and gases from their bodies, had continued to maintain a slow burning, but high intensity heat source, long after the bulk of the oxygen in the room had been used up. As the heat source was contained in their direct vicinity, and once their bodies could no longer supply any more fuel (once all of the wax had melted away from the candle, as it were), then the fire was finally extinguished.

"I hope this will serve as a warning to people everywhere, as to the dangers that exist within our homes. Please think carefully before deciding to self medicate. Always stick to your doctor's prescribed dosage, and never mix alcohol with your medication. Please, please remember that items such as electric blankets should be turned off at the mains, before you get into bed at night."

By Robert Smith – Assistant News Editor.

I stared at the article. My body felt numb.

"Sally and Jacob," I said, for no particular reason other than I owed it to them to say their names. I casually flicked through the other papers in the file, convinced I had seen the worst of it; it was only then another clipping caught my eye.

The Leicester Clarion - Wednesday, August 26th, 1987

Heartbreak in Leicestershire village as tragedy proves too much for Claybrooke fire husband.

THE close-knit community of Claybrooke is in shock and mourning for the second time in less than six months, after the tragic death of Mark Featherstone. Following calls from concerned family members at the weekend, the emergency services forced their way into the home of Mr. Featherstone, who lost his wife and child earlier this year, following a fire at their home in the Leicestershire village.

Mr. Featherstone's body was found in the bathroom of the two-hundred-year-old cottage, which he and his wife had lovingly restored. It is believed he had taken a combination of tablets and alcohol, before climbing into a hot bath and cutting his wrists.

A close family friend has confirmed that twenty-nine-year old Mark Featherstone had been suffering from depression and that he had been receiving counseling; in an effort to help him cope with the loss of his wife and child. The friend also announced that a note written by Mr. Featherstone, addressed to his parents, had been found at the cottage.

A spokesman for Leicestershire police has confirmed the incident is not being treated as suspicious and that they are not looking for anyone else in connection with Mr. Featherstone's death.

Mr. Featherstone is survived by both of his parents and two older brothers.

By Staff Reporter.

My head dizzied. I closed my eyes and attempted to suppress the barf that had risen in my throat as I read through the second article. It was bad enough finding out a woman who I had sat down and held a conversation with was actually a ghost, and even more than this, one who had suffered a horrendous death... but, to then discover that her husband had drowned, or else bled to death in a bath... Memories of the horrific events at the culmination of my recent *traveling* returned, slamming into my mind with the force of a sledgehammer crashing through the back of my head. Could this revelation about Mark's death be a bizarre coincidence? My *traveling* experience had happened just hours after sitting down and talking with Mark's *dead* wife. How could it not be connected?

Furthermore, I had been visited by a woman who it turned out was dead. Wasn't this insane, anyway? The horrors I had witnessed made me wonder; was it possible that Sally Featherstone was somehow trapped by this place, forced to relive her own death, and that of her child, over and over again. The situation was made even grimmer by the fact her husband had chosen to take his own life just a few months later. It seemed likely that the turmoil of these deaths was a catalyst for the haunting of the cottage. I couldn't be certain of any of this, but there was one thing I was certain of; for some bizarre reason Sally Featherstone had managed to step away from this place. Fate brought her to my door, and even though she probably didn't understand the true nature of the situation she was in, she had literally begged me to help her and her family. Well, I was going to do my damn best to help them.

"A penny for your thoughts, Jack?"

I looked up, surprised I hadn't heard Linda and the Stauntons entering the room. I smiled at my wife.

"I was just thinking that it's all going to be alright."

"Really?" she replied, sounding more than a little surprised. "You're certainly sounding more chipper than you were fifteen minutes ago."

Faye handed me a steaming mug of coffee, which I attempted to take a sip from; but all I succeeded in doing was scalding my lip. Still, and despite wincing from the pain of the burn, the mug itself supplied comforting warmth in my hands.

Faye joined Marcus, and their still sleeping son who he seemed reluctant to unhand, and settled back into the sofa. Taking a sip of her coffee, she gestured for Linda to take a seat in one of the adjacent armchairs. Then she pulled a packet of cigarettes from her pants pocket. "Anyone?" she offered.

We declined in unison. Linda had never smoked, and I had been required to quit after losing a lung in the accident. As distasteful as I found her choosing to smoke in front of the infant, I have to admit I could have used a drag. My nerves were shot.

Faye shifted position so that she was directly facing me.

"So, Jack, it's been a hell of a day so far, right?"

I attempted another sip of the coffee, this time managing a small swallow before the burn hit the back of my throat.

"You're not wrong," I said. "Hell of a day."

Marcus was sitting quietly, just staring down at the picture of contentment cradled in his arms. Without warning he suddenly looked up; the events we had witnessed seeming to have weathered his features impossibly. He looked to have aged maybe ten years in just the few hours I had known him.

"How the hell is this possible, Jack? We all saw what happened up there. Hell, you and I both got burned. Yet moments later it was as if nothing ever happened. We wondered what the score was with this place when we first bought it. The reason why it had been standing empty for so many years? To be honest, we have had all sorts of weird shit going on around here from day one; but nothing like what happened today. What the hell does it all mean? Linda says *that woman*, Sally Featherstone, she visited your home. How the hell is that even possible?"

"I don't have all the answers, Marcus," I replied. "All I do know is that Sally and her son, maybe her husband too, for all we know, would appear to be trapped here in this place. As improbable as it sounds, they may not even realize they are dead. Based on the things Sally told me when I first met her, I think she thinks it is *you* who are haunting her family. Remember, to Sally Featherstone, Misty Ridge is *her* home. I think her finding me was a cry for help, on some unconscious level."

"So what the hell do we do now then, Jack?" Linda asked.

"Now, my dear," I replied grimly, "you get your wish, and I call Violet…" Even as I spoke my mind was rerunning the events we'd witnessed, and I knew that char grill would forever be off the menu.

Ten

Events at Misty Ridge had proven traumatic beyond imagining, so much so that we returned home and immediately uncorked a bottle of red – which eventually turned to three-and-a-half bottles as we lamented the day's events late into the evening. Hence, following a night of drinking heavily while trying to digest the insanity of the day's events, I never got round to returning Mother's call until the following morning. I expected a tongue lashing for having kept her waiting, but her mood proved surprisingly affable. However, she was adamant we needed a face-to-face. I promised I'd call round later that day, and then quickly bade farewell.

Linda wasn't in the best of moods before I left the house, largely because of revelations I'd made the previous night. In her mind I had been keeping secrets, about my astral travels, and regardless of my reasons for choosing to do so, my wife was feeling betrayed. Still, I was in no mood to be lectured by a parent, and so the sun was at its highest before I reached my mother's three-storey brownstone.

I pushed open the gate – the dropped hinges causing rotted wood to drag on leaf layered flagstones – and edged my way sideways up the garden path. Passing once immaculate borders, now grown to threatening Triffids, I reiterated to myself that the place was long past Mom's upkeep.

My father died six months before my accident, an undiagnosed aneurysm claiming him as he slept in his favorite Victorian-wingback. It came as a horrendous shock to all of us, but my mother has never fully recovered from the swiftness of his passing. For reasons I still didn't comprehend, she almost immediately began filling their once pristine home with tat bought from yard sales, boot sales and second hand stores. Born of a generation who still found worth in daily tabloids, I doubted she had discarded a newspaper in the last several years.

Helen, my eldest sibling by five years, now lives in Düsseldorf, but neither she, nor husband Graham, ever tire of badgering Mom about the need to sort it out. It reached the stage where every phone call ended in their having a spat, and their relationship has now dissolved to a once fortnightly check-in to confirm Mom is still ticking and kicking. Not much of an input, but still a damn sight more support than Emma ever offered. Eighteen months my senior, my darling sister, Emma, skipped the family nest while I was still in school. She has pretty much spent the last twenty-five years drinking and screwing her way around several of the world's continents. She didn't even make it home for Father's funeral…although she did remember to send a card. Last I heard she was shacked up with a twenty-two year-old in Thailand. She's a real class act.

Linda and I also make regular intimations about Mother having a *serious* sort out at the house. Our softly-softly approach annoys Helen no-end, but it's okay her keep stirring the pot from the comfort of another time zone; she isn't the one has to deal with problems on the *old* home front.

I rang the doorbell as I slotted my key into the lock. "It's only me," I called, pushing past a half-dozen carrier bags littering the floor, and doubtless filled with new yard-sale acquisitions.

"I'm in the kitchen," Mother's reply echoed through high ceiling rooms. "You want a coffee?"

"Please." I moved crablike through to the lounge, edging sideways past four-foot tenements of newspapers – each stack bundled with yellow or blue twine – and an abundance of garments, male and female clothing drooped over hangers, displayed three deep on any available support. The lounge too was a maze of stacked papers, although in this room the summits of various columns were in use, piled high with a sundry of charity store clothing. Two (now barely visible beyond the mountains of tat) units rested against the far wall, and these, along with the marble shelf over the fireplace, bore a crowded mass of china, brass, and glass ornaments, along with numerous photographs – many displaying faces unknown to me, and just as likely unknown to Mom too; frames bearing images of complete strangers, ghosts discarded by history, purchased from a dusty shelf in some tacky seconds store.

I squeezed onto the sofa, parting a stack of officious looking papers from the multi-colored pile of bedding rested alongside them, and carefully slotted myself into the space between, just managing to melt into the seat as Mom entered the room, bearing a fully laden tray.

I moved a twelve-by-sixteen, wooden lockbox – in which I knew my mother stored objects bearing sentimental value – to one end of the table, and after some further maneuvering of old magazines, and a battalion of plastic WW2 action figures, Mom finally succeeded in setting the tray down on the coffee table nestled between the sofa and her favorite wingback (the chair being the only uncluttered object in the room).

Mom set two mugs of steaming black coffee onto coasters, and then sliced us both a portion of chocolate gateau. "I bought this from Judkins, yesterday afternoon. Best cake shop in town."

I took a bite of sugary sweet – melt in the mouth – chocolate sponge. She wasn't wrong in her assessment. We soon devoured a second slice of cake, even before finishing our coffee, and then spent the next twenty or so minutes indulging in idle chatter. I asked how she had been keeping, and whether she had spoken with Helen recently. She assured me she was feeling tip-top, and that she had enjoyed a lengthy telephone conversation with my sister, who had now promised to stop criticizing her lifestyle choices. Mom then asked how Linda was, and whether the summer heat was suiting my aches and pains, or perhaps aggravating them. It's a strange situation, but there is never any constant with regards to how fluctuations in the weather affect my wretched joints. Extremes of heat can prove as unpleasant as extremes of cold, and yet, on other occasions a baking hot summer's day can supply a soothing massage, bringing relief to my ills.

It is fair to say my visit had so far consisted of pleasantly idle chitchat. It is also fair to say that Mom insisting we needed a face-to-face alerted me to the fact this wasn't likely to remain the case.

As she returned from the kitchen with refills of coffee, I realized I was about to find out just why I had been summoned. "So then," she said, setting the mugs on the low table, "how did the case go?"

"The case?" She had doubtless realized I was working, purely based on her previous day's conversation with Linda, but I knew she lacked any details. It would be best if this remained the case.

"Come off it, Jack. Linda more or less admitted you were working. Give me some specifics."

"There wasn't much to it. It's hardly worth bothering talking about, really."

"A boy should know better than to lie to his mother."

"I hardly qualify as a boy, anymore."

"You'll always be my *little boy,* Jack."

"Nevertheless, there really isn't much to tell you. A woman suspected her home was haunted, but it was all very mundane really."

"You're twitching like a dog with a tic. You never were a good liar, Jack."

"Mom... I promise."

"Okay... Good. Mundane is good, right?" I could almost hear the cogs whirring in her brain as I sipped my coffee. "So, you haven't suffered any recent experiences involving bathwater?"

I coughed drink down my shirt, staring at Mother with wide eyed disbelief as I spluttered and choked.

"You okay? Do you need me to pat your back?"

I held up a palm to indicate things would be fine once the coughing fit subsided.

She waited until I composed myself. "I take it that's a yes, then?"

"You've spoken with Linda," I accused.

Mom shook her head. "Not since yesterday."

"Then how?"

"You really need to ask?"

I looked into my mother's eyes, trying to read what really lay behind them. Each and every time she *guessed* a truism, Mother always insisted she had *the sight*. This wasn't a claim I remembered much of from my younger years, although to be fair I recalled very little with clarity from those times. It wasn't unknown for my mother to *nail* facts on something of which she should have little knowledge, and she had certainly offered unexplainably accurate forewarnings, previously; the Dresden house sprung to mind.

I had always taken these claims with a pinch of salt, assuming they were a little poke of fun at my decision to set up as a psychic investigator.

She was serious.

"Oh my God. You're being serious?"

"If anything, I don't tend to get as many flashes as I did when I was younger, but the alarms still tend to sound whenever you or your sisters are in harm's way. The night you almost died I became hysterical, even before they were cutting you out of the car. It was me who called Linda to say there had been a dreadful accident."

I nodded. "I know. Still baffles her. She puts it down to a mother's intuition."

"Maybe that's all it was."

"You don't believe that."

"I've been around for a lot of years. I've seen a lot of precursors. The afternoon your father died, I knew something bad was coming. I still hate myself for not seeing it was him in danger."

"Don't do that. It wasn't your fault."

"The aneurysm? I know it wasn't, not directly. But I loved your father, and after all those years together I should have been able to do something to save him."

"Mom. Please, don't."

She forced a half-smile. "You are right. This isn't the time for moping reminisces. I need you to tell me what you're involved in."

"Why such concern? And more to the point, even with my shaken and stirred brain, how come I've made it into my forties and I'm only now realizing my mother is psychic?"

"You readily accepted it when you were a child, as did your sisters."

"They did? *We* did?"

"Sure. I was born into a family of two brothers and six sisters. I was daughter number seven. My mother too, she was her parents' seventh daughter. I'm a seventh daughter of a seventh daughter. I guess I was always going to have *the sight.*"

I thought of white haired, saturnine faced Grandma Sprig, and realized my mother was aging into a slightly rounder version of her own mother. "I always thought the sight was supposedly reserved for the seventh son of a seventh son?"

"The world used to be a whole lot more sexist."

"Damn." Could my mother really be psychic? It seemed improbable, but then again, probably no more so than my own astral adventures. How could I have forgotten so many things from my past? That bloody car crash really messed me up.

"Tell me about the case, Jack." The request was issued with a surprising degree of worry. "Tell me everything."

I rescinded the previous decision to keep matters to myself, and instead spent the next thirty or so minutes describing every insane detail of the events unfolded at Misty Ridge. It was something of a rarity for Mom, but she managed to sit quietly throughout, listening intently, and offering little more than an occasional shake of her head, or perhaps shifting forwards in her seat. At times her eyes displayed a concern bordering outright terror, so much so that I avoided mentioning my astral travels. She would have been aghast.

At the culmination of my tale I asked Mom's opinion. Already the passing hours had made such events seem less-and-less likely, and now, speaking the words made it sound even more absurd. "I know it sounds like insanity, and I know my brain got the whole piñata treatment during the smash-up, but it wasn't just me who experienced these things…"

Mom slumped back in the chair, nodding as she did so. "I believe you, Jack."

"But it's over now, so no need for such concern."

She shook her head, and although I may have been mistaken, I thought I saw her shoulders tense and she tried to halt a shudder as she spoke. "I doubt it'll ever truly be over for you, Jack."

"Why would you say that?"

"I think there is a dark force that seeks to hold sway over you."

"Say what? What the hell sort of comment is that?"

She let out a resolute sigh. "When the girls were small, and you were a still a baby, we bought a small terraced house in Lloyd Road. It was only ever a stepping-stone property. We intended being there for eighteen months, tops. Plaster the walls, slap some paint around, turn a profit and move on."

"Okay?"

"We decorated the two smallest bedrooms first. Not in kiddy colors, but still, nice pastel shades that any future buyers wouldn't be offended by, and decent quality, hard wearing carpets through both rooms."

"Where are we going with this?"

Mom chose to ignore my question.

"You were still sleeping in a cot at that stage; a lovely looking piece, mint green color, with a drop side, and a metal sprung base, and decorated with kitsch bears displayed in various entertaining poses."

"I don't see what this has –" she silenced me with a wave of her hand and a sternness I had all but forgotten.

"Hear me out, Jack. This might be important, okay?"

I nodded apologetically and she continued on, seemingly unaware that her mentioning of that cot had stirred something unpleasant, a memory buried deep within the recesses of my mind. It was lost to me, at least at first, but even then I sensed it was something inhumed for my own wellbeing. Ice ran through my veins. I sipped at my coffee, hoping it would offer some comforting warmth. Instead, as mother continued recounting her story, and despite my taking a second swallow of suddenly unexplainably-bitter coffee, in the hope it might quell the revulsion rising through my gut, memories long forgotten began sweeping over me; my jaw clenching as tight as my buttocks, I closed my eyes and failed to banish a long forgotten, though now rapidly returning nightmare –"

It is the height of summer and I am warm, perhaps bordering on uncomfortably so; despite being stripped to a cotton bodysuit and layered only with a thin blanket–which I have already kicked below my knees. The glow offered by the nightlight is gentle, orange-pink even through closed lids, and the distant murmurings of the downstairs television, along with the occasional sounds of laughter–my parents, talking and laughing in tones which soothe–comforts me, and gives reassurance of their close proximity. I fidget from my side onto my back, and something tickles the top of my thigh. The lightness of the contact induces an involuntary giggle, and a second movement, lower down my leg, is greeted with the same response. Something scurries across my cheek and down my neck, and suddenly I am frightened. There are things crawling on my legs and up my arms, and even through the cloth of the bodysuit I can feel their weight pressing on my chest. I attempt to open my eyes, but thin legs tangle with fine lashes as they rest upon my lids like coins of the dead.

I scream with an urgency that reveals my understanding of true terror, with cries so frenetic it causes the unseating of whatever rests atop my eyeballs, and as the fiends climb down from me, one of them crawling over my lips, briefly dipping into my mouth as it does so; I look to the blur of movement shrouding the ceiling, and even as a black wave begins sinking towards me, the bedroom door is thrown wide, and as light floods the room my mother screams, her cries echoing my own in the face of the descending wave of black spiders...

"Jesus. Fucking. Christ." My cup lies on the floor, its spilled contents soaking the already stained carpet. I was shaking uncontrollably, and even though my mother moved to embrace me, still I trembled.

"You remember?"

"Those spiders –"

"I hadn't got to that bit yet. It makes no sense that you could remember…you were far too young."

"Those spiders. Those dirty fucking spiders. All over me."

She cupped my face and maneuvered me towards facing her. "Jack, it wasn't the spiders. They weren't the problem."

"What do you mean they weren't the bloody problem? Christ sakes! What are you talking about?"

"Jack. You obviously haven't remembered everything, but then how could you? You shouldn't even be able to remember as much as you seem to have. I promise I'll explain everything, at least as best I can. But please cut the profanity, okay? You weren't raised like that, and this is my home. Show some respect to your mother."

I nodded, apologizing as I did so. My mom was right. I wasn't usually one for using major expletives but, damn…those spiders.

"Tell me what little you remember of that night?" Mom urged, as she made a return to the wingback.

"Spiders. Black ones. There were hundreds, maybe thousands of the things, abseiling through the darkness, multitudes of tiny ninjas descending out of the night. They were all over me, dozens even before the lights came on."

"No," said Mom. "You're wrong...at least partially and certainly in your interpretation of events."

"How so?"

"Those spiders...I think they were there to save you."

"What...? That's insane."

"What else do you remember?"

"Someone picked me up. It was Dad, I think. I remember being scooped up from out the cot, and then someone frantically brushing bugs off of me as I was hurried from the room. Someone was screaming."

"That was me. I was the one doing the screaming. It was your dad got you out of there."

"So why do you say the spiders were there to save me?"

Mom took a deep breath and nestled into the chair. "Your dad and I, we were watching *The Tommy Cooper Show* on *ITV*–such a funny man, it's a shame the world lost such a talent. He really was a genuinely unique individual –"

"Mother. If you wouldn't mind..."

"Sorry, dear...but, such a shame. Anyhow, the show had cut to a commercial break and I had just put the kettle on to make a cuppa. That was when we heard you screaming. You were never a child who cried a lot, not then nor later; but that night, it sounded as though Satan himself had come to steal you away. If any of you kids ever cried during the night, one or other of us would volunteer to sort things out. That night...we both knew something was seriously wrong. Almost tripped over each other getting up those stairs...and when we got there..."

"Go on," I urged. Mom's features had visibly paled; memories of a horror which, even after so many long years, still plagued her.

"I was first to reach the landing, but only by a few steps, and even then only by grace of the fact the kitchen was next to the stairwell. I'd never heard cries like it, and by then the girls had woken and were screaming too, although thankfully they never had any idea as to the horrors occurring in the next room."

"Tell me about those horrors."

"I pushed open the door and right away saw the spiders, their webs glistening like mist under the backdrop of lighting from the landing. There must have been a thousand of them, or more, descending like a black shroud towards your cot; but as unsettling as that sounds, it wasn't until I turned on the room light that I saw the true horror."

"Go on." My flesh was crawling and perspiration leaked from every pore. I knew I was close to learning something I would be better off not; but I needed to know.

"Roaches. Your tiny body was covered, head to foot with cockroaches. Not as many in number as there were spiders, though still likely several hundred or more. Your face, legs and arms were already covered in little red welts where they were nipping at your flesh, while all about them others were scattering; like proverbial roaches under room lights."

"Jesus Christ." Ice water ran through my veins and sweat prickled my cheeks and lower back. "Roaches?"

My mother nodded as remembered disgust etched her features.

"But how? Why? It makes no sense."

She shook her head. "How or why, I don't know…but I have a theory, at least so far as answering one of those questions goes."

"I'm listening," I said, urging that she continue.

"That night, after we'd given you the once over, just to check there were no serious bite wounds, or roaches playing hide-and-seek inside your outfit, I took you into the girls' room. We spent the night in there while your father brought a chair up onto the landing. There he stayed, making sure nothing unpleasant exited your room, and being only seconds away from me and you kids–should we have had need of him."

"And?"

Mom attempted a comforting smile, but her eyes betrayed her. "And, nothing...all remained quiet, for the rest of that night and for every night after...although we sold up quickly, barely avoiding a loss, but we were out of there within eight weeks. After what we had seen, being free of that house was a blessing."

"I'm not denying it was a terrible and disgusting thing that happened, and certainly more than a little odd...but, still, an infestation of various bugs doesn't really qualify it as being of supernatural origin."

Mom gave a disdainful snort. "I think that's your *paranormal detective* head talking. Perhaps you should allow me to finish up, and then see if you can still say it wasn't beyond odd."

I could see my response had stung Mom, and so I made a conscious decision to avoid cutting in again, at least until I was sure she had finished.

"The next morning, your father called work and reported he was sick. There was no way I was staying in that house alone with just you and Emma, thankfully Helen had started school by then. Your father telephoned Environmental Health, told them we had a major bug infestation, although we decided it was best to leave out the finer details of the event–we realized it would have sounded crazy. However, reports of a virtual plague of roaches, this was always going to incite a response, and their man arrived before three that same afternoon. He was a little fat chap; with a big head and wide chops–looked a bit like a miserable hippopotamus. Bill Travis was his name, and, as it turned out, he was a very pleasant man. Although, being honest, when your father and I talked him through the previous night's events, he looked at us like we had fallen out of our tree.

"He said he would check around downstairs first, after which your father took him upstairs and showed him each of the bedrooms. He wanted to check for signs of infestation in other areas of the house. Thankfully, he pronounced us as being clear. Finally, he looked in your room, and this confirmed the scenario was as we described it.

"The mattress in the cot was layered with tiny bodies, the flooring too, all but obscured with a multitude of dead insects, like dropped leaves in the fall. Bill was gobsmacked. He had never seen a sight that in any way resembled this. I made him a cup of tea while he grabbed two refuse sacks from his van, and then he meticulously collected up the two variants of bug, counting each one as he bagged them. He gathered up 295 cockroaches of the *Blattella Germanica* genus. The presence of the spiders – which he identified as being *Tegenaria atrica,* the giant house spider, a venomous though generally placid family of spider – surprised him considerably, because they usually only enter homes during the cold seasons, and even when they do, it is never in such abundant numbers. The spiders numbered 367 dead bodies."

"Jesus. That's a lot of dead bugs. It's a wonder I don't have a rabid fear of arachnids. But what killed them?"

Mother was giving me her harshest, most disdainful look. "You still aren't getting it, are you? Those nigh on seven-hundred little corpses, they were just a fraction of the creatures entered your room that night. They were the victims of war."

"War?"

"Yes, war. The roaches were attacking you, nipping and biting your flesh. The wave of spiders, we later realized they must have crawled down from the loft, entering the room through gaps we found in the ceiling plaster, they arrived to protect you. We realized this on the night, even as it was happening. As soon as we opened the bedroom door we could see a battle being fought, a fight between insect races. The roaches' intent on sinking their jaws into your soft pink flesh, the spiders possessed by some unrevealed guidance, driven only with a solitary purpose, a need to attack the vermin assaulting you. I would guess the dead numbered barely a third of those engaged on each side."

I sat motionless. My mother was talking crazy-talk, and yet…

"What did the bug guy say…Bill, was it?"

"He wrote it up as a freak event, something unlikely ever to happen again. He assured us the house was critter free, but still he promised to drop by when he was in the area, just to check we were still unburdened. He called round at least a half-dozen times over the next three weeks."

"And?"

"And nothing. There was barely an insect to be found, and certainly nothing like had occurred previously."

"And yet still you wanted out of the place?"

"Do you blame me? The damage had been done, at least as far as I was concerned. I had no foresight you were in any kind of danger, and this bothered me greatly…but I understood you wouldn't be safe if we stayed in *that* house."

"But how can you know that, really?"

"I just do, okay?"

"It still makes no sense. As bizarre an incident as it may have been – and I'll agree it was that. There is nothing to suggest a dark force was involved, or that said force had, or has intentions on me, is there?"

"Jack, what do you remember of our time at Madeline House?"

"A little, but not a lot…then again, I don't remember a whole lot with any clarity from way back then."

"But you remember Old Black, right?"

I smiled. "Of course." I didn't remember much from those years, but I remembered a house of uncomfortable cold spots, and incidents of objects seemingly moving by themselves. I also remembered the old dog. He was my first best friend. My parents had begun making some healthy money with their property renovations, and we moved into another virtually derelict home in need of my parents' TLC. I was about five years old at the time they purchased Madeline House, a red-brick cottage, situated in the village of Old. The first week we arrived, my father spotted a dog, a black lurcher of indeterminate age, wandering across fields at the back of our property. A neighbor later informed him the dog was a stray. It had been wandering the area for several weeks, and was presumably getting by on the abundance of wild rabbits.

Dad decided to leave our field-gate open, and he started putting out scraps and a bowl of fresh water. Mom chastised him, saying the leftovers would encourage foxes, but it took less than a day for the dog to discover the offerings. It didn't take long for my dad to encourage some interaction from the animal, and before the end of that first week the dog had demonstrated affection and loyalty, particularly towards the males in our household – a fact which somewhat irked my sisters – and Dad and I declared him a member of our family. We had no idea of the animal's true age. Although full of bounce his muzzle was graying, and so Dad suggested we name him Old Black – a black dog, found abandoned in the village of Old. Thinking back now, the naming may sound a little corny, but as a child I'd thought it hysterically clever.

I looked at Mom, noting her features appeared both weathered and sad, as though unburdening herself of such a long held secret as the bugs; it had only intensified her woes. She gestured towards the lockbox. "Jack, be a good lad and pass me the box, would you? There is something I think you need to see."

I reached for the receptacle. "Why did you ask what I remembered about Madeline House, and about Old Black?" I said, handing the carton onto Mom's lap.

Grimacing as she did so, my mother opened the box...

Eleven

Mom raised the lid and slid her hand inside the box. From my position on the sofa I could see the container was full almost to the brim, as congested with treasured memories as the rest of the house was with clutter. With the carton balanced in her lap, Mom's hands disappeared into the stored paraphernalia, rooting through old photographs, pulling out and setting on the table several strips of colored ribbon, a blue garter, book markers, a small wooden elephant, and a dozen or so other pieces that held some intrinsic value. It was with a degree of satisfaction when finally she succeeded in her quest, pulling forth several pages of yellowed notepaper, folded into quarters. Keeping the box in her lap, she reached across the table, her extended arm offering me the notes.

"What is this?" I asked as I relieved her of the papers.

"Just read what's written down, Jack. Then we will talk some more."

I unfolded the sheets and realized I was looking at a child's scrawl...but more than this, I knew this handwriting. I looked at my mother.

"Yes," she said. "You wrote that poem. You were barely seven years old at the time."

My eyes flicked across the pages. "As I recall, I was something of a late reader. Besides, how could a young child have written this, or set it down in such order?"

"Please, Jack, just read the whole thing, and then we will talk about the words on those pages, and the events of that weekend."

There was a lurching trepidation in my gut as I turned my eyes back to the old papers, and the poem entitled *Black*.

Black

Little Jack watched as Father closed the bedroom door,

After saying, "goodnight my son,"

And Jack buried his head beneath the sheets, and prayed that she would not come.

Hideous hag in long dark dress,

She entered his room each night,

To mutter and curse in unspoken verse,

And fill his heart with fright.

Jack decided to stay awake,

As he had on every night which came before,

But eventually eyes flickered, then closed,

And his worry was no more.

Around the witching hour,

He awakened with a start,

Icy fear clambered up his spine,

And grabbed hold his beating heart.

Bedroom door slowly opens,

The rooms filled with a blue grey light,

And young Jack could tell, it was different now,

She had come to claim him on this night.

Jack doesn't want to go,

He desperately tries to resist,

But her cold and bony fingers,

Cut deep into his wrists.

She leads the boy from bedroom,

Along winding landings to the stairs,

And when at the top, then she did stop,

To gloat that finally he would now be theirs.

Icy fingers gripped tightly onto Jack's shoulders,

Getting set for one big push,

And just as she was to launch him,

To send him flying through the air,

A low guttural roar, and then the sound of paws,

Moving ever closer up those stairs.

From the darkness, the shape that emerged was Old Black,

A lurcher, of good age and spirit true,

And although that dog sensed evil,

He never doubted what he should do.

Old Black moved quickly toward Jack,

Once side by side they grew strong,

Old Black's canines bared and gleaming,

Little Jack's fear now gone.

Now that dark woman spat out,

That she would have her way,

She raised her hands and versed silent bands,

But that old dog did not sway,

No matter what she tried this night,

From his boy he would not stray.

Suddenly, Old Black leapt forward,

And with one mighty canine roar,

He sank his teeth deep into her,

And dragged her to the floor.

With one last silent scream of rage,

That dark woman she was gone,

Old Black had banished her,

Back to where she did belong.

As Jack climbed back under his covers that night,

He felt so safe, secure,

With his old friend beside his bed,

Lying stretched out on the floor.

When Jack's eyes opened, it was morning,
He squinted as he saw the light from the sun,
He leapt up, and raced to his parents' bedroom,
To tell of all that Old Black had done.

Mother sat up in bed, as she heard her boy come charging in,
She said, "Come and climb in here my son,
While we tell you of some things."

As Jack climbed upon their bed, Father cuddled him,
It was with reddened eyes, and between deep sighs,
But finally Father did begin,
"I'm sorry son, but me and your mom,
Well there's something we must say,
You see, at half-past-seven last night,
Old Black he did pass away,
He was just lying by the fireside,
And peacefully he slipped away.
I know it is sad, but we should just be glad that..."

"No! No! No!" Jack did protest,

"This cannot be right!

You see Old Black he came to me,

It was dark, it was late, and it was night!"

Well they said Jack was dreaming,

That he had imagined all which came before,

But I know what Old Black did that night,

Yes, I know what I saw,

He was there for me,

To care for me,

To stand right by my side,

Without you my faithful old friend,

Evil would never have been denied.

For a long time I just sat and stared at the papers in my hands, not wanting to lift my head lest Mom saw the tears welling in my eyes, emotions stirred by the partial recalling of something that insisted on remaining at the periphery of my memory. Finally, without shifting my gaze, I pressed for answers. "You have to tell me."

The lockbox was beginning to weigh on Mom, and she edged it off her lap and onto the table, her gaze never leaving me as she performed the task. She brushed a hand over her lap, straightening her frock, and then melted back into the chair. With a casual wave she gestured towards the notes I clutched. I held them tightly, as though in fear some crazy gust was about to sweep through the room and permanently steal them away from my grasp. "You wrote the poem the afternoon after Old Black died, which is odd enough really, because you're right, you were a late reader. A year after you had wrote those words, you could still barely decipher a Ladybird book. All very odd."

"And the content?"

My mother declined making eye contact, choosing rather to let her gaze sweep the room. "From the get-go, it was another strange house. There were always sudden and unexplained cold spots cropping up, and we'd sometimes get up in the morning to find objects moved about the kitchen work surfaces. At first your father suspected we had a rat, and this particular rodent had a propensity to rearrange coffee jars and canned goods – though never showing any intent to rifle the contents therein.

"But then things got even weirder.

"Larger objects started being moved about the lounge, armchairs, coffee tables, even the sofa on more than a few occasions."

"And this didn't concern you...given the previous event with the bugs?"

She shook her head. "It wasn't the same...at least not at first. These incidents weren't happening everyday, not even what you'd call regularly. And it never felt threatening...not then."

"So what changed?"

Mom ran a finger along the pale white scar that traveled from her right brow to her scalp. "This was the start of it."

"You always said you got that in a fall."

She smiled. "I was standing on a chair, hanging new drapes in the girls' room."

"And you took a tumble?"

"Something grabbed my ankles, totally upended me then smashed me face first into the windowsill."

"Maybe you slipped."

She grimaced. "Your father suggested the same until I showed him the finger marks around my ankles, indentations applied with enough pressure it left bruising lasted a fortnight."

"Jesus."

"And that seemed to be the start of it – the start of the worst of it, at least. Objects began moving with far more regularity. You became convinced that some creepy old woman was entering your room at nights, whispering awful things at you. At least three times a week you'd wake up screaming and terrified. There were cold spots so intense we often sat with our coats on, even when the heating was firing. Old Black took to spending more and more time outside. It got so we used to leave him in the yard when we went out, otherwise he would just cry and howl nonstop if left inside. That dog took a real dislike to the house, and so did I."

"What about the girls?"

"The girls were fine. Sure, they occasionally saw objects moving unaccountably, but they were at an age where we were mostly able to laugh it off as a *friendly ghost*. They never saw any of the real unpleasant stuff. Even the cold spots seemed to avoid them. I suppose it's quite bizarre really. But then they were never the target."

"And you believe I was?"

Mom fixed me with an icy gaze. "I'm convinced you were. We had already seen enough, the property was on the market before Old Black passed. Unfortunately, the move came too late for that old pooch."

"What happened?"

She gestured towards the papers in my hand. "That night went down pretty much as you described it, at least so far as Old Black just lying down and passing in his sleep, and us telling you this the next morning."

"And the old hag?"

"Well, you certainly came charging into our room insisting someone or something had tried to take you away, and that Old Black saved you."

"But you didn't believe it?"

"Even with all that had gone before, it seemed doubtful."

There was something in her eyes. "But?"

"The landing carpet was wet underfoot, right at the top of the stairs where you claimed Old Black had fought with the hag. Closer inspection revealed it was damp with blood; quite a lot of blood."

"Whose blood was it?"

"Your father and I checked all three of you children. Not an abrasion to be found, although you had bruising around your left wrist; looked just like finger marks. We had wrapped Old Black in his favorite rug, placed him in the conservatory where it would be cooler; intending to give him a proper sendoff in the morning. When your father checked the dog's body prior to burial, he found its flesh layered with deep gouges, its muzzle and teeth stained with blackened blood; it looked as though the animal had been in a pit fight; except none of that made any sense, because we had both been in the lounge when Old Black died. We were watching a movie, and the lazy mutt was doing his best impression of a bum beside a campfire." Mom emitted a gentle laugh. "It's a wonder that dog never ended up cooked, how near he used to lie to the fire."

I smiled, my eyes now as watery as my mother's, but I couldn't find the right words.

Mom took several deep breaths and dabbed at her tears with a tissue. "I'm not quite sure how it went down that night, or even on what level of reality, but I believe you owe your life to that dog. He was a good friend to you; to all of us, actually."

"You've never mentioned any of this before."

"How could we? You were a child; hence we laughed it off for the sake of both you and your sisters. We were out of that house within three months of that night, and besides, the mind works to avoid trauma, and so it didn't take long for those events to be pushed into sealed recesses. It is better to leave some things buried."

"So why tell me now?"

"Because this course of action you have chosen, embracing contact with the *otherworldly,* I feel you may be opening yourself up to something dark; something unpleasant that has a purpose for you."

"That sounds like nonsense. I'm not disputing the disturbing connotations of the events you've described, but there is nothing to suggest I am the prey of any such thing."

"On at least two occasions you have been targeted by something I can best describe as evil, and on both of these occasions a power of light has presented assistance. I believe a war is being waged over your soul, Jack. Something has you marked for a purpose."

"Mom. There is no war being waged. You think I have the Devil on my back, and God battling to dislodge him, so that I may serve the light?"

"The light? Have you never read the Old Testament? Bah! Angels and demons are just two sides of the same coin, and much like in each and every war that came since, it was the victor who got to prescribe history."

"You know you're sounding certifiable, right? What you're saying is absurd."

"I'm well aware it sounds crazy, Jack. I'm also sure that much of what I've said; at least to anyone else, it would seem like the ravings of a mad woman. But I'm your mother...and you know I'm not nuts. I'm just saying, Jack, there's a whole lot more going on here than you might care to believe. So you shouldn't be too willing to trust anything that you think you know. These *things* that have plagued our family, they seem to get their kicks from loitering around your life. To them it's all just a game...and the game is always on their terms."

"So you think we are all just puppets having our strings pulled? More importantly in this instance, you're suggesting I'm the pawn, who for some obscure reason has been earmarked?"

"Aren't we all being played on some level? Look at the atrocities being inflicted throughout Europe over these last weeks. Do you believe the people carrying out those acts get out of bed in the mornings with any desire to be *wicked?* It's no different than the devastation our young men inflict on the Middle-East, under orders of various men purporting to be Christians, supposedly acting in the name of righteous and just causes. These *crusades* usually revolve around regime change for control of state assets, not for any *good of the people*...and let's not forget there is *always* money to be made from the act of war, itself. And it isn't even just about war. Across large swathes of this world people are starving to death and being blighted by disease or catastrophic events of nature. Does any of this sound like the work of a loving God? I have no idea which deities actually exist, or if *any* of those quoted in scripture are real. Either way, I doubt there is any one of them could claim to be the *true* Lord Almighty. It is probable we are all just pawns in the hands of some pretty dispassionate cosmic beings, and that, while to some of these *gods* we are at best insignificant, to others we are worth tormenting, rejoicing like spiteful boys exhilarated at pulling the limbs from a daddy longlegs. Their true purposes are likely something way beyond our imagining – although it seems not unreasonable to suggest they relish overseeing our pain and suffering. We are little more than plastic soldiers, waged in a war between boy gods. Trust me, son; you need to ask yourself how far you wish to travel down this rabbit hole."

Twelve

I had a lot to mull over as I left Mom's house. On top of everything else discussed, I never before had her pegged either as blasphemous or a conspiracy nut...or perhaps she really was just downright crazy? Either way, I hadn't realized she was so well read on subjects esoteric. There was obviously more to my mother than I ever imagined. The woman had also shown grievous concern over my pronouncement that Misty Ridge rested amid a bed of slate and magnetite. These two metals are apparently both gateway minerals, capable of opening portals to other realms. The two together, and in such abundance, it was impossible to know what possibilities they offered; though it certainly added to my mother's woes.

Prior to visiting, I had decided against mentioning my out-of-body experiences – particularly with regards to Morocco – and this I felt had been a wise decision. Otherwise Mom's concern would have been without bounds.

It had been probably a couple of months on from the accident when I first got round to describing to Linda my habit of popping out from my body. It is fair to say she had been skeptical, at least at first–a skepticism that later became troubled disquiet – her initial assumption being that I was suffering med induced hallucinations. Convincing her of the authenticity of my *travels* had proven surprisingly easy. I persuaded her to select half-dozen articles of clothing, and to lay them out in the garage once I had retired to bed. She then hid the garage key, just in case I decided to pull a fast one. The next morning, not only had I been able to identify the various garments, but also to describe their precise location within the building. Linda's mood shifted rapidly; her initial surprise and elation quickly souring to concern over the dangers of vacating my corporeal body. It would be reasonable to say she's never since been enthused with the idea of my astral travels, which is why I tend nowadays to just avoid the subject. This time, though, upon our return from Misty Ridge – and encouraged by the copious amounts of wine we downed – I had felt she was owed a fuller explanation of all that had gone before; including the incident involving the bath. My revelation horrified her, even more so because I had been keeping the details of these regular sojourns to myself. Her initial anger turned quickly to tears, and I am sure the situation wasn't aided any by the earlier events at Misty Ridge. Nonetheless, I was angry with myself. I had previously refrained from revealing all to Linda, but only because I didn't want to worry her. But the foundation of our relationship was openness and honesty, and on this occasion I had kept my lips sealed. I hated the thought that, because of my keeping secrets, in the future Linda may doubt my integrity.

Thankfully, Linda seemed to have regained some composure by the time I returned home. She appeared her usual fun and cheeky self, although given the nature of events the previous day, I suspected her manner was little more than a mask, worn to try and raise my spirits.

Later that evening I telephoned Violet, giving her a rundown on everything that had occurred; beginning from the moment I first met Sally Featherstone. Violet reacted like a five-year-old on Christmas morning, her fervor rising as I informed her of our experiences at the cottage. She could hardly wait for an opportunity to visit with these *happenings*.

I always knew she was a little strange.

Violet offered to cut short her trip to Manchester and return home immediately, but I managed to persuade her she should honor family commitments before making a return. It was with a degree of reluctance, but eventually my psychic sidekick agreed to stay and finish her business up north.

My mind remained busy right up until I retired for bed that evening. My mother's revelations had weighed heavily upon me, although I didn't realize quite how heavily until I slept that night.

Thirteen

I am floating in a seemingly endless void, and at first the only view on offer is a blank canvas, black in its entirety. Slowly though, as my eyes grow more accustomed to these surroundings, I realize there are tiny spots of light, capricious sparkles in far away galaxies, offering just enough hope I am not alone. I come to the realization this is a lucid dream, for not ever have my travels permitted me such distances, and neither have they instilled such fear as that permeated by this blackness and isolation.

The scene shifts, and I realize there is now a planet floating mere miles beneath my feet, in its entirety it is a ball of gloomy red. I decide to take a closer look, and so descend through red clouded heavens until my feet scuff down in carmine dirt.

I stand on this world of melancholy dusk, its plains flat and barren beneath a sky washed with purples and reds by a seething black sun. It is without regard of the fact I see no signs of civilization, because still I sense only deprivation, isolation and loss. I look miles distant to a swollen pimple that rises on the land, a pink blister marking its otherwise smooth skin, and I feel drawn to investigate.

As is always the case within dreams, and unaffected as I am here by disability, I close the distance in mere moments, and am surprised to discover the truth of this scene; what I had thought a speck of imperfection, it proves not a solitary blight upon the landscape, but rather a range of mountains so tremendous their peaks are all but lost amid carnelian clouds.

I stand in awe; each of these behemoths would surely dwarf Everest, perhaps by a ratio of ten times or more. Then I notice the rift. A split in the mountainside; a gash cut so deep it runs from summit to base, and it renders a seam wide enough for passage. I embark on what seems an endless path, clearing between obsidian smooth faces of stone laced with veins of red mineral; the ground is sharp underfoot, and offers enough width for a solitary, uneven passage; between crevice walls as cold to the touch as a lamppost on a December morn. I am overwhelmed by a fear that some unknown force might yet compel this breach to slam shut, crushing me as assuredly as a mosquito caught between the pages of a closing encyclopedia. It is with major relief I spy the approaching red slit before me.

Realizing as I do that I am nearing the end of the pass, I stride out in haste to complete this route, and soon thereafter step clear of the gorge. As I do so my jaw slackens in awe at the circle of mountains encompassing me. Their height appears even more grandiose from my current location, the silence and desolation of this place both overwhelming and intimidating, and I feel as a gnat...nay, as a flea, when looking up towards a man.

The amphitheatre of mountains in which I stand is enormous, creating a symmetry approaching perhaps ten miles or more through its diameter, but there is also something else...

Rising at the very center of this clearing, a cone of misty jade light stretches skyward, and although miniscule in comparison to the range, it appears to house a sizeable structure.

Once again I stride out, overwhelmed by the need to identify something unidentifiably familiar. Due to the irrational laws of this lucidity, it takes me only moments to cover half the distance I seek, but then I am stopped in my tracks by a realization. I had thought these mountains simply topped with lofty peaks, but a casual glance through breaking red cloud surprises me. I see a figure stories high, its effigy carved into the very pinnacle of the mountain off to my right...and it stands not alone. I strain my eyes, trying to determine exactly what it is I am looking at, and then a bell of revelation chimes.

During my recuperation period, Linda had bought me a book on ancient deities, as she rightly guessed it would be something of interest to me. I had thoroughly enjoyed reading about all those gods of yore, but the cleverness and savagery of the Norse,

Greek and Roman deities; it garnered a particular fondness within my heart. I stare skywards, towards the figure wearing a Viking helmet and old time Scandinavian tunic; he holds in his right hand a drawn sword, while his left embraces the Gjallarhorn – the Resounding Horn – this figure represents Heimdall, ever vigilant guardian of the Aesir. Alongside him stands another giant carved of stone; his handsome features further enhanced by a smile that seems to stretch wider than his face, and the rock from which this figure is carved...it is glowing. Faintly, and barely noticeable unless staring directly at it, but the image gives off a yellow aura, and this light is the only thing offers any hope in this place. I am drawn towards recognizing this man as Balder, also of the Aesir. He is a son of Odin.

The mountain is rimmed with effigies in rock, and it is not alone. As I survey the crowns of the other peaks, I see other figures; men carrying warhammers or bedecked with thistles and crowns; women, half-human half-bird, or part serpent; men with fish-tails, elephant-heads, dog-heads, and men with bat-wings, and still there are other creatures too; multi-limbed monstrosities and dragons, giant wolves, owls and spiders...the spider, it is Anansi the Ghanaian god of stories. They are all gods. Framed in stone; over-watchers of this place; though for what purpose?

I wonder if perhaps it is Mother's denouncement of such beings, that they are not the true lords' of always, perhaps has drawn me to this place.

I have no further time to ponder. The structure shrouded at the center of the jade mist, it continues to grow, sprouting forth from the ground at an alarming rate; Jack's beanstalk rampant on steroids. I press on, forwards towards the commotion watched over by these stone gods.

As I draw closer I realize the mist surrounding the structure is alive with pulsating lights. At first I think them blinking with various shades of green, but soon I realize it is the fluorescent mist that colors them so. Just occasionally one of the erratically moving objects will slip clear of the rising steam of jade, and whenever this happens I am amazed at the quivering spheres, each one is an egg of rainbow luminosity large enough to birth a grown man. They seem capable of not just lightning fast movements, but also having an ability to disappear amid fizzling crackles and pops of energy, before reappearing mere instances later, though having traveled great distances away.

It is truly stunning to watch them dance flamboyantly across red gaseous skies.

I continue to move forward, until for the first time my eyes are able to make out some of what is occurring within the rising chute of green hue. The structure within appears of metallic construction, and from a wide base it continues to narrow over the course of its climb, although at its summit it seems incomplete. Given the nature of its curvature, I had expected its zenith to come to a needle sharp point; instead it is an open

153

flower of twisted and burning metal, the top struts of its frame flattened and distorted, budding out into fiery petals atop the stem of this steel organism. Many dozens of bugs tumble from near the apex of the stalk, blackened silhouettes falling, or perhaps having chosen to jump, clear and away from the burning crest of this alien structure – but these lemmings have failed to note the base of the tower, for this too now blazes with flames that lick skywards, like glowing tongues reaching to accept falling morsels.

I have been so engrossed with observing the structure; I had failed to notice the orb hovering away to my right. Bobbing gently in the air, like an angler's float on placid water, it is settled perhaps forty feet in the sky above me, pulsing steadily, it gives off a resonance which for some unexplainable reason delivers an impression the thing is observing me. As I turn and my eyes meet it, it begins to move in my direction, descending as it does so until it stops several feet in front of me, quivering with inconceivable energy as it loiters no more than a few feet above the ground. I can see a shape beginning to form inside the ball, suggestive of rapidly growing spawn in a gelatin sack. Within moments the figure stands fully formed, and as She presses her face to the membrane that restrains; I can do nothing but admire Her features.

She pushes a leg free of the still pulsing, fizzing capsule, and it emits a loud pop as She steps from within the dazzling globe. As

She does so the light behind Her seems to evaporate away into a single point of energy, and although not in any traditional sense, I see She is gifted with beauty beyond imagining.

Her hair hangs loose across pale shoulders; it is as white as driven snow. She stands inches taller than any average man, although the trimness of Her figure belies a normal woman. She wears an off the shoulder gown the color of pearl, the material of which pulses and resonates, becoming translucent enough to glimpse Her small breasts and smooth contours.

I am enamored.

And then She smiles.

Her lips curl to an unpleasant grin, causing marble cheeks to raise and dimple beneath eyes of black oil. Her teeth are straight and impossibly white, and for a moment serve to further enhance Her allure...until the stench of death and decay begins to assault my nostrils. Each breath She takes releases halitosis of putrid demise. I am forced to step away, suddenly stricken by the realization of what this being standing before me represents. She points a slender finger in my direction, and the cruelty of Her smile confirms She condemns me. She opens her arms wide, palms raised towards the sky, and as She does so two more spheres crash to the ground. One either side of Her they splash onto the floor, each fizzing and glutinous mass spreading out into a puddle sized ooze of rancid decay. I watch in terror as a thick muscled arm rises from beneath the surface of the gooey pool, and I am certain She has summoned my death. The creature climbs clear of the bog, even as its twin begins to crawl out of the second placement, and I see horrors beyond possibility.

These manimals, for surely there is no other way to describe such beings, stand twelve-inches or taller than any normal man. Their flesh is newborn-pink, though visible only through a matting of coarse white hairs; the ears, set high atop the head, are erect and pointed, and the head itself elongated towards a blunt snout, each side of which is lined with ferocious looking tusks easily capable of goring a man. Each of their limbs ends in four toes; each central pairing offering certain death, with claws the length of steak knives.

The creatures move forward until standing one either side of Her, each squealing and grunting porcine urgency as they eye me with cruel intention. It is only once She opens her mouth and screams words I cannot fathom, unleashing death breath that makes me want to drop to my knees and puke, then do Her hellions fall to all fours and begin their charge.

I turn with urgency, noting that the sliver of dark creasing down through the mountainside, identifying the route of my passage; it suddenly seems so far distant it will surely be beyond my reach. Still though, I run as fast as ever my limbs will carry me.

But it is no use.

I here snuffling guffaws and squeals closing at my heels, their excitement barely containable as they hunt me down. Though I sense they are toying with me, they close the initial distance so easily; for sure they can take me whenever they please. One is right upon me now, I can feel its breath on the back of my neck...I will die in this place...I will die in this place...I will die –

"Jack? Jack? You need to wake up, Jack!"

I open my eyes to a comforting vision. Linda's face appears as a picture of concern slowly coming to focus through the well of my tears; her smile is one of relief tinged with worry. "Jesus Christ."

"You were dreaming."

"I think it was more a nightmare."

"I couldn't wake you."

"Why not?"

"Don't know. I've been trying to shake you awake for the last five minutes. I knew you were dreaming. I'd been lying here listening to you mumbling on for perhaps ten minutes or more, than you started getting all twitchy and stressed. You ended up screaming like you were terrified, but even then I couldn't get you to wake up."

I mopped a damp hand across my wet brow. "Fuck."

"Do you want me to get you some water?" She began to roll away from me as though to get out of bed, but I swung my arm round her waist.

"Just hold me, Linz. Just hold me for a minute, okay?"

Settling onto her side, she draped an arm and a leg across my body. "Eeew! You're all damp."

"Sorry love. Perhaps I should grab a towel."

She moved her face closer to mine. "Perhaps," she said, stroking my face, and then guiding my mouth to meet her own.

"Uhm," I said between snatched kisses, "and what's going on here, Mrs. Keswick?"

"Well, Mr. Keswick, you're all damp, remember?" She kissed me, attempting more fervor.

I pulled away, slightly. "Yes, I'm still a little moist." I whispered. "So, what's your point, exactly?"

She shifted position, untangling my embrace and moving to straddle my pinned and supine body, then leaning closer to nibble and whisper into my ear. "Well, Mr. Keswick, seeing you getting all panicked these last few days…makes me realize just how much I love you." I felt her hand reaching lower, passing down beyond my waist until she found the object of her affection. "Besides, fair's fair, hubby of mine," she said, guiding me towards her, "you're not the only one who's a little damp."

I kept my eyes open, focusing entirely on Linda as she moved astride me, because every time I closed my eyes the woman from the red world was gloating over me.

Fourteen

Unlike the majority of events in my life, that recent dream, and the landscape on which it occurred, has maintained clarity, both in its detail and the despair it brews within me. I hope it is a thing eventually forgotten, and for sure that day cannot come soon enough.

Violet finally returned to Northampton two nights ago. I offered to pick her up from the train station, knowing this would allow me an opportunity to discuss events in greater detail. As I sat in the car listening to the radio, news began breaking of a thwarted terror attack on the Channel Tunnel. Security forces had detained six men, with at least two more suspects shot dead at the scene. The media were reporting that police had since made another dozen or more arrests in the Greater London and Birmingham areas. The world really did seem to be descending into chaos. *Could Mother be right? We are all being played.*

I silenced the radio as I spotted Violet exiting through the station's main doors. She had experienced enough tragedy these last few days. The woman is a (at times infuriating) bundle of effervescence, and is rarely, if ever, quiet, but as I climbed from the car to greet her, she seemed nothing like her normal self. Her mood was as grim as the weather, although, in fairness, she had been in the city dealing with her late aunt's estate.

Cancer had taken Violet's mother when the girl was just five years old, and Aunt Clara had raised her from that day forth. Even for someone convinced of continuation beyond this life, I could see the hurt glazing Violet's eyes.

As I waited outside the station, the sky had begun rumbling and flashing; with the threat of a storm that finally broke as we drove home; the unleashed downpour reminiscent of that night on the motorway. I gripped the wheel tight with both hands and tried to blank out all thoughts from that night, but I can't deny the inclement weather felt like a portent, a reminder of my mother's words, and a warning against my return to Misty Ridge.

Rain battered the car, but Violet seemed almost oblivious to the horrendous driving conditions. She listened passively as I talked of the events at Misty Ridge, her eyes once-in-a-while drawn to following the rapid tick-tock of wiper blades across the windscreen. Only occasionally did she ask a question, and then without any insight or conjecture. I began to worry about the timing and magnitude of this case.

As we drew up outside the three-storey, Georgian terrace Violet calls home, the storm had abated to a tolerable trickle. I decided to voice my concerns. She replied with a forced smile, and then, as I helped carry her bags from the car to the hallway, she patted my arm and assured me she would be more like her old self following *a good night's rest.*

As I made to leave she called for my attention, and I returned to where she waited on the porch steps. "Jack…are you okay?"

"It's been a helluva week so far."

"That's not what I'm asking."

"What then?" I asked with genuine confusion.

"You seem…different. It's as though there is darkness loitering over you."

"Really? Cheers for that." *Like I'm not feeling crap enough, already.* "As I said, been a hell of a week."

She nodded and touched my arm. "Goodnight, Jack."

I walked back to the car, and as I turned the key in the ignition and waved goodbye, I considered a silent prayer to any higher power prepared to listen – but Mother's words still haunted me, and so I decided against encouraging whatever it was she felt still watched me.

Driving home, I considered the situation. Violet is a good friend, and although I hated seeing her so down, she remained a damn fine medium. However, if we were going to resolve whatever was happening at Misty Ridge, it would require Violet being focused and having her head fully in the game.

Fifteen

I climbed out of bed bright and early. Truth to tell, I had been awake since about 3am, perhaps daunted by expectations of whatever lie before us. I called ahead to inform Violet I was on my way, and by the time I arrived at her place she was waiting outside on the porch, a ridiculously large brimmed sun hat hiding her curls as she enjoyed the clement morning. I was relieved to see a familiar smile now painting her features, and it quickly became apparent she had found some degree of internal balance; perhaps *knowing* there is so much more than *this*, it had at least helped to ease her loss? *Or perhaps it was a guise chosen with the purpose of bolstering my own faltering prowess?*

Either way, I guessed I would find out soon enough. I had little option other than to let the day play out.

As I pulled away from the curb, Violet raised a ginger brow: "No Linda?"

I shook my head. "No Linda. And I'm not surprised given events the last time. She has decided to sit this one out. I can't say I blame her."

Thankfully, Violet really did appear more at peace with the loss of her aunt, and she spent a portion of the journey talking of the woman, and also recounting tales of her own childhood in Manchester – including how it had been Aunt Clara's thrice weekly trips to the local spiritualist church which initially piqued Violet's interest in the departed. During the remainder of the journey Violet quizzed me about Misty Ridge – and in a manner more inline with what I'd expected the previous evening. The greater the questions she asked, the more at ease I felt; Violet was an exceptionally gifted medium, and it was reassuring to know she was up for whatever waited ahead. I contemplated sharing my mother's revelations and suspicions, but decided against doing so.

Some things are better left unsaid.

The sun was already a blister in the clear blue sky, and the motorway stretched out before us, shimmering like Quetzalcoatl's plumage, a silver feathered-serpent whose back we now rode towards destiny.

Even though I have never once had cause to doubt Violet's capabilities, my stomach churned as we took the slip leading towards the A5. Fifteen minutes on from this, as the sound and bustle of heavy carrier traffic faded into the distance, we enjoyed the favor of a more sedate road. Violet shifted in her seat until she was looking directly at me. It felt as though she was scrutinizing my every feature, and I flashed a disconcerted look. After a few uncomfortable moments, her words turned to my astral travels – with concern specifically devoted to the Moroccan bath incident.

"You say you've found yourself in that particular town at least six times?"

"Yes. Six times, now. And it always ends up at that house."

"And you have no idea why? You have no previous affiliation with that town, or even with Morocco?"

"None whatsoever."

"And you've definitely never been there on holiday? Or even considered it as a holiday destination?"

I shook my head and steered a sharp left towards Claybrooke. An expanse of labored fields had opened out on either side of the lane, but the land to out right remained completely flat, and this allowed for a splendid panorama which painted itself across the horizon. "As best I can tell, Foum Zguid is a desert town more inclined to hikers and sightseers. Can you honestly picture Linz humping a backpack across the desert beneath a blistering sun?"

It was Violet's turn to smile. "I get it; she's more of a pool and pina colada type girl, right?"

"You didn't have to be psychic to know that."

"I certainly didn't." Violet laughed. "You're a lucky lad, Jack. You've been batting way out of your league for years."

"Oh, trust me, I know that. Even carrying this gimp leg, I can't deny I struck the jackpot with that woman."

Violet mulled things over for a moment before returning to the subject of the house in Foum Zguid. "Your experiences in Morocco, Jack, something is calling you to that place."

"That sounds like something my mother would say."

Violet smiled. "It sounds like your mother is a wise woman."

It was my turn to smile. "I wouldn't go that far."

"Okay. But, seriously, something is pulling you towards that place."

"But what, exactly? And, more importantly, why me?"

"Why you; this is something I cannot explain. As for what exactly may be drawing you to Foum Zguid, well, I suspect this is easier to answer. It's the woman. Aya."

"Aya," I repeated, and as I did so I was immediately overwhelmed; my head spinning with the grief, loneliness and despair she suffered prior to ending her own life; I once again felt the sting of the blade at my wrists, blood covering feminine hands and thighs; and then, suddenly, water; slipping lower in the tub, the bath waters turning crimson from open wounds, and the liquid beginning to fill my lungs; a woman's resolute acceptance of encroaching death replaced by the stricken, blind panic of a man who, suddenly, realizes he is afraid to die. I slew the car to a stop in the middle of the lane, afraid I may otherwise lose control of the vehicle.

"Jack?"

"Jesus. What the fuck just happened?"

"What did you see?"

"I was there. I was back in Foum Zguid bleeding to death."

"And then?"

"And then I was somewhere else, someone else...bleeding from the wrists, but this time I was drowning, too."

Violet nodded knowingly. "I can't be one-hundred percent certain but... this *someone else*."

I mopped a hand across my brow. "Yes?"

"I think you already know the answer."

"Mark Featherstone."

She nodded. "It's a cry for help. I don't know why, or even how you were approached, or even the reason these two scenarios would both be playing out like this. It's strange enough to think that a dead woman, Sally Featherstone, visited your home and asked directly for help...this alone takes some crediting. It seems too much of a coincidence; your impressions of being in the bath must surely be connected to Misty Ridge, and Mark Featherstone's death. Though how any of this directly relates to the Spirit of Aya, or why she also appears to be reaching out to you..."

"So you've got nothing?"

I think Violet could hear my disappointment.

"She needs your help with something... Perhaps she needs *you* to assist her in moving on?"

"What? That's crazy. I sure as hell don't know how to help with anything like that. She would have been better off contacting someone with similar abilities as you."

"Spirits often work in mysterious ways, Jack." She attempted a reassuring smile, although I felt as though she was weighing me up. "I suspect there is a link between Aya and the events at Misty Ridge. I know that doesn't seem likely, but it's my best guess for now. Maybe, just maybe, our sorting out the one situation will lead to a resolution of the other?"

I found Violet's assessment less than convincing, and even less reassuring, but for now I was left with little choice other than to put Morocco on the backburner. I shifted into gear and floored the pedal. Claybrooke lay ahead.

Less than five minutes later we rolled onto the forecourt at Misty Ridge, to be greeted by the sight of Marcus loading a picnic basket and blanket into the back of a Nissan. He waved an anxious greeting. Faye joined her husband as we exited the vehicle. She was drawing heavily on a filter tip, the inch of burning ash hanging from its stem betraying her anxiety. After some brief introductions, Faye proceeded to strap young Peter into the Nissan's baby seat.

Handing over the keys to the property, Marcus informed us we could have the cottage to ourselves for as long as we might need it, as the family were setting off for a picnic they would make last the whole day. It appeared to be with some haste they climbed into the vehicle, and Faye called out to us that we should help ourselves to anything we may want. She had left us a platter of ham and pickle sandwiches in the fridge, and there was also a six pack of sodas. Then, with a less than hearty wave, they reversed down the drive, their pallid faces revealing a truth beyond the pleasantries as they rode off into the distance. I looked at the rotund, gaudy little woman alongside me, her purple caftan billowing like drapes under the slight breeze.

"You ready?" I asked.

Violet had dropped to a stoop and was examining a handful of magnetite rocks which she collected from the loose soil. She was grinning like a cat that has just got the cream.

"Always ready." She beamed.

I felt more relaxed than I expected in returning to the property, perhaps as I now had the support of my *psychic superhero-sidekick* – although, truthfully, whenever things get to a certain level, it is I who is actually the sidekick. Anyways, disregarding the issue of whether I am Batman or the Boy Wonder, I pushed open the door and stepped across the threshold, as a cool serpent coiled in the pit of my stomach.

Violet noticed my manner and gave a playfully indignant snicker. "Surely you're not going to squeal like a baby *again,* are you, Jack?"

I stopped in my tracks and turned, eyeing her sharply. I desperately wanted to think of some waggish retort, but words failed me – I so wished I hadn't divulged the full extent of the distress I suffered during that previous visit. My rotund little helper was never going to let that one go.

"Come on, hero." She smirked, giving me a sharp dig in the ribs.

I followed inside, trailing behind as she wandered through each and every room in the cottage, meticulously scrutinizing every facet of the different areas. Neither of us engaged in conversation as Violet walked the rooms, picking up and inspecting various artifacts, running her palms across flat surfaces and down walls and drapes; getting a feel for the place. Occasionally there would be a sudden halt in proceedings, usually followed by Violet raising her palms and declaring something to be *interesting.* I never queried precisely what it was she found interesting; I knew better than to ask questions at this juncture. Violet can be wonderfully entertaining, a real raucous bundle of fun, but while she is working, when she is doing her stuff, Violet is all business.

Eventually we found ourselves returned to the lounge. Violet was standing in the centre of the room, palms up, and arms stretched wide, nodding assertively as she pronounced – somewhat theatrically – "This is the place. They are focused here."

"Here in the cottage?" I puzzled.

She shook her head. "No, they are here in this room." She gestured for me to remain quiet. "By the power of good and all that is right, by the spirit that is love and with a touch so bright – you came forward asking for our assistance – so I call to you now, to step forward into the light... Sally. Come to us, Sally. We know you are here. Be with us now."

I waited with baited breath as Violet repeated the mantra thrice more. After what seemed like an age, from behind us came the sound of a woman's voice. I'll be completely honest here; even Violet jumped slightly as the arrival caught her unawares; me, I nearly soiled myself.

We turned to find ourselves facing Sally Featherstone, who was standing in the doorway leading from the kitchen. My eyes dampened at the sight of this young woman, whom I had watched being incinerated. And yet here she now was, standing before us looking fit and well, or at least *well* by her standards. In truth, she looked drawn and tired like a woman who hadn't slept for days, but this was still a better look than the last time I saw her – burned to an ebon char.

"Hello, Jack," she said, smiling. "I'm so glad you came. And it's nice to see you've brought a friend with you. You are both welcome."

"Hello, Sally," I said. "It's really, really good to see you again."

She looked at me, a somewhat puzzled expression on her face. "Jack, are you okay? You seem a little upset."

I shook my head. "No. I'm fine. Everything is going to be fine."

Her smile returned. "That's good."

With an open palm I gestured towards Violet. "Sally, this is an associate of mine. Her name is Violet Day. She is a psychic medium, and I asked her to come here today so that she can help."

"Excellent." With a look of genuine relief playing across her features, Sally turned to face Violet. "So, you really think you'll be able to help us with all this weirdness? Help us put a stop to all of the odd crap that has been going on around here?"

Violet gave a gentle nod and smiled warmly. "Yes, Sally. I'm going to help you. All of you."

"Thank you, so much," Sally replied.

I realized at this point something strange was happening (although doubtless it was no weirder than conversing with a woman I knew to be deceased). Sally appeared to be losing the exuberance with which she originally greeted us. She no longer smiled and, as I stared at her, color drained from her features leaving a pallid complexion reminiscent of the time we met on the landing.

"Are you okay?" I asked. Quite probably a stupid question to ask of a dead person, but she really did, all of a sudden, look dreadfully unwell.

"I'm fine," she said. "Although to be honest, all of this business is beginning to get me down. Feel free to carry out any investigations around the cottage that you need to, but I'm afraid you'll have to excuse me for a while. I'm going to take Jacob upstairs and see if I can catch a little snooze."

I looked on dumbstruck as I realized Sally was holding her sleeping son. I was sure that moments earlier the child had not been present. Furthermore, her last words instigated a sickening déjà vu in my gut. I glanced at Violet, who appeared just as surprised as me by the infant's sudden appearance. Sally crossed to the foot of the stairs before Violet regained composure enough to speak.

"What is it exactly that is beginning to get you down, Sally?" she asked.

Sally turned and faced us, a look of incredulity straining her features.

"What? Are you serious? Hasn't Jack explained about all of the weird shit happening around here?"

Violet nodded comfortingly. "Yes, luv, he has. But I don't know what is wearing you down the most. Is it the paranormal happenings in your home, or the lack of sleep and the situation with your husband?"

"What do you mean?" asked Sally, averting her gaze.

"You know what I mean, Sally," Violet asserted. "But in order for me to help, I need you to open up and talk about things. Can you do that?"

Sally closed her eyes and nibbled at her top lip. The first time I met her she had looked drained to the point of being spent; this figure looked a shade of that feeble woman.

"I really do want to assist you," Violet affirmed.

Sally stepped back into the room, although seemingly with some reluctance. She was making snuffling noises, and tears had begun streaking her cheeks. A dribble of mucus trickled from her nose. Using the sleeve of her cardigan she wiped her face, and quickly resumed nibbling her lip.

"It's okay, sweetheart," said Violet, reassuringly, "in your own time."

"It's not fair," Sally began; her voice barely a whisper. "We used to be so happy. It's just that, since Jacob was born, I feel so tired all of the time. And now, with Mark working nights, well, we just keep arguing all the time. I think that maybe he doesn't love me anymore. I'm just so very, very tired all of the time. I can't seem to get a decent night's rest; I think because of the horrible dreams I keep having, and all of the other weirdness."

Violet smiled reassuringly. "Tell me about those dreams, Sally. Is it the fire you dream about?"

Sally's mouth fell open; her crumpled features enlivened with vigor as she turned to face Violet.

"Oh. My. God. You really are a psychic. Did you read my mind or something?"

Violet was shaking her head.

"No. I only know about the fire...about what happened to you and Jacob, because Jack told me."

"I don't understand," Sally said. "How would Jack know about my dream?"

"No, Sally. He doesn't know about your dream. Jack knows about the fire because he, along with Faye and Marcus Staunton, witnessed it."

"You're making no sense. He witnessed what, exactly? It was a dream. And who are Faye and Marcus Staunton?"

"Faye and Marcus are the people who live here now. The fire, it was a terrible, terrible tragedy. But it really is time for you to let it go. It's time for you to find some solace. You deserve to be at peace."

"What are you saying?" Sally said; although her tone suggested that somewhere deep inside herself she already knew the answer to the question.

Violet's eyes misted as she gazed at the young mother and the small boy content in her arms.

"Let me tell you what I think, Sally. Or rather, what I feel. Over thirty years ago, there was a great tragedy happened in this place. It wasn't anyone's fault – certainly not yours. You were a young woman, trying her best to be a loving wife and mother. I think perhaps, like many women who find themselves in similar situations, that without obvious reason, at least not one easily identified, you began feeling depressed.

I don't doubt you tried your best hiding this depression, certainly from those closest to you. In fact, you likely felt guilty even feeling this way. And then, once Mark started working nights, your moods darkened even more."

Sally remained silent, her eyes staring straight ahead. She was standing so motionless; I couldn't even perceive her breathing, assuming of course that spirits do actually breathe. Then, and for only the briefest of moments, it looked to me as if Sally and her child started to fade away. It didn't last long, but I could swear their forms became intangible as a morning mist, and then, just as readily as it started… it stopped.

I told myself it had been a trick of the light, but it was a thought that proved as incorporeal as the woman and child. Something else was happening. Both were emitting the subtlest of glows; something I can only describe as an aura of vitality. For the first time since I set eyes on Sally Featherstone, the woman was radiating a spirit and energy more readily associated with the young; she looked healthy and alive. Sally stared deep into Violet's eyes, and then, finally, she turned her attention to me. Tears were tracking her cheeks, running along her jaw and down onto her neck, but nevertheless she maintained a smile as she spoke.

"I think, Jack, that maybe your friend is very good... Since Jacob was born I have felt so low, but I shouldn't feel this way, I know I shouldn't. I have a loving husband and a beautiful son. Yet I get so angry at Mark for leaving me alone at night, and even more so since all of this weirdness started. It's got to the stage that now, when he is here, all I seem to do is pick fights with him."

I knew this was my cue; I had to ask.

"Sally, when did you last argue with your husband?"

She considered the question for a moment.

"This'll sound a little strange, but I'm not sure."

"Of course you're not, dear," said Violet. "It's all just remnants."

"What do you mean?" Sally and I asked in unison.

"This place," explained Violet, throwing her arms skyward, and sending the huge sleeves of her caftan fluttering like washing in a breeze. "It's all just debris from the hurt and tragedy having taken place here. What happened to you and Jacob, in the fire, it left an impression on this cottage. As did the marital strife you were having with your husband. It's like making a recording on one of those old cassette tapes. An imprint remains long after the original event. One that can be replayed even after the precedent becomes a lost narrative. You have been trapped here; day after day reliving a tragedy for which you hold no blame, those same affairs played out again and again, for more than thirty years now."

Sally looked stunned, at least momentarily…then she laughed.

"You're not seriously trying to tell me I'm dead, are you? That I'm just some sort of video phantom, acting out lines in a daily soap. That's absurd."

"She's got a point actually, Violet," I said. "I mean, Sally came looking for help. She sought my assistance because she felt the cottage was haunted. She's here talking with us now, for Christ's sake. How can something you say is trace impressions, simply an *imprint* of psychic energy, hold rational conversations?"

"It can't," Violet replied. "Or at least it couldn't, if that's all that was happening here. Maybe I haven't explained myself very well. Events of a highly stressful or significant nature can quite easily get stamped onto a certain place. These are basically recordings of the past, left behind. Sally, try to remember something you were doing earlier today, before we arrived. In fact, try to remember any significant event has happened of late. Other than arguing with Mark, or going to bed and dreaming about the fire, what can you tell us of your life?"

"That's easy," Sally replied indignantly. "All sorts of odd and crazy things have been happening around here. This is why I went to Jack for help in the first place."

"Exactly," Violet said. "The trauma you experienced would not by itself have been enough to keep you earthbound. As I said, it would just create an imprint, a ghost, if you will. But you, my dear, are a spirit, which is something altogether different. You are trapped here, but only because you have unfinished business."

"This is nonsense. If I'm trapped here then how did I manage to go seeking Jack's assistance?"

"Well, to be honest I should imagine that was just a fortunate coincidence, really," replied Violet. "Perhaps you can answer a question for me. What would you say if I were to tell you that Jack's address is 137 Greengage?"

"What?" Sally looked as though she was about to lose her breakfast.

"I don't get it," I said, looking at the growing concern on Sally's face. Her response, when finally it came, was barely audible, but I was just able to decipher the words.

"That's my parents' address," she said.

"I suspected it would be something along those lines," Violet said. "Sally, you are a sentient being, who is basically trapped on a continual roller coaster of unpleasantness. It is a ride you have been forced to experience over and again, for more than thirty years. I believe that once the Stauntons moved into this place it acted as the catalyst to, for want of a better phrase, wake you up. You only recollect fragments of your life here; nevertheless, those were enough to have convinced you it was the Staunton family who haunt this home.

"The fact you ended up seeking help at Jack's address, a house where years ago your parents lived? Well, I guess we have to put that one down to a lucky coincidence. Or, perhaps, *fate* would be the better term. Either way, it was a good thing, because it's going to help you and your loved ones move on from this place."

Sally's face was a blank slate devoid of expression. It was impossible to gauge just what the woman might be thinking, and the tone of her voice offered even fewer clues. "Let's just assume for one moment I choose to believe you, about my being dead – and I honestly can't believe this is a given. But assuming I accept the things you say; you said that I, we, are stuck here because of unfinished business. So what exactly is this *business?*"

Violet smiled warmly. "You know the answer to this already. Sally. Be honest with yourself. What is the one thing you want more than anything else?"

Sally closed her eyes, shoulders trembling with emotion. "I want Mark...I just want Mark to love me the way he used to."

"Of course you do, dear. Of course you do," assured Violet, clasping her hands together as if in prayer. "The thing is, Sally, Mark does love you. He always has, and always will. I know this to be true, I feel it. If you can bring yourself to trust me, well, I would like to try and show you just how much Mark does care."

"Jack?" Sally's eyes pleaded a need for reassurance. As I think back to that one moment, it fills me with certain contentment; a young woman, who had suffered through so much, and yet was willing to place her trust in me.

"It'll be okay, Sally," I said. "Violet is a good person, and she knows what she is doing."

Sally's response was a barely perceptible nod. "Thank you, Jack."

"Excellent," Violet clapped. "Sally, would you mind letting Jack hold Jacob for a while, please?"

Sally's eyes flickered a moment of uncertainty, and then, she quietly passed her sleeping child into my arms. The boy didn't stir. As I looked down at his smooth features and wispy hair, I noticed for the first time that he shared his mother's coloring. I then couldn't help but wondering, was the infant perhaps in some permanent state of catatonic slumber? Was this how it had been ordained, that he should spend eternity sleeping peacefully while his mother continually relived the same nightmare, over and over again?

Violet's voice returned my focus. Turning around I saw she had moved, taking a position directly in front of Sally. She took hold of Sally's hands, gently sandwiching them between her own. Violet recited a prayer of some description; however, hers is a voice carrying the long term wear of 50 cigs a day and her words deliver with a distinct gravel tone. I could barely make out anything of what she was saying. In truth, I am not entirely convinced she wasn't speaking in tongues. Although, much later, when I asked if it had been some version of Latin, or perhaps another less known scripture she had been reciting, she just laughed and punched my arm.

Violet continued on with the supplication, each time repeating the same verses over and again, never stopping the unrelenting mantra until, gradually, a change began to impact the cottage in which we stood. It began slowly, at first barely even perceptible, but there was just the faintest inkling of the gloom hanging over this place starting to lift.

Over the course of the next several minutes, as Violet continued her narrative, the change became more palpable. Perhaps the best way I might describe it is this; if you have ever walked into an old building for the first time, and almost instantaneously realized you have fallen in love with the place. It is an emotion stirred by the very fabric of the build. A positive imprint of its history etched into every facet of the edifice; you just know you could stay in this place, living out the rest of your days happy and contented within these walls. This was the demeanor which settled like flakes of snow upon the Staunton home. Sunlight painted small cottage windows, offering a wash of illumination far more pronounced than upon our arrival, and certainly greater than during my previous trip to the cottage; no longer was the light restricted to a dreary bleed through colorless panes. Windowed rooms now basked in sunlit verve. Such was the sense of melancholy lifted it is difficult to fully rationalize, perhaps other than to suggest that whatever ills previously afflicted this place, they had now been replaced with something heartier. The cottage held a wonderful, *healthy* feel.

It was then, as I rejoiced at the sense of pain no longer hanging over this place, I realized Violet had stopped the recital. Both women were staring, wide eyed and in my direction.

"What?" I asked, hairs rising on the back of my neck.

"Thank you. Thank you so much," said Sally, tears once again tracking down her face.

"What?" I repeated, still perplexed.

"Turn around, Jack," said Violet, a big self-satisfied grin playing across her features.

I did as Violet requested and turned around, which resulted in my nearly suffering heart failure. I found myself face to face with a dark haired man; he was of stocky build, and exhibited the same pallid complexion Sally had displayed for the majority of time I had known her. The fact he was standing so close to me and yet I hadn't in any way sensed his presence, well, let's just say that, if I had been a farmyard chicken, the experience may have induced the laying of an egg. I took a step away and almost fell ass-over-tit over the coffee table set alongside the sofa, but for the sake of the child in my arms managed to save myself, and in so doing avoided further indignity; although I can't be sure as to whether anyone else even noticed my embarrassing break-dance. Violet's gaze was fixed firmly on the young couple, and they had eyes only for each other. Tears streamed down Sally's face as her dead husband held out his open arms to embrace her. They came together, kissing with tender passion for what seemed an age. Finally, their lips parted and Mark turned to face me, smiling as he set eyes on his sleeping son still content in my arms. I stepped forward and with gentle care handed the child to the anxious father, and as I did this the boy opened his eyes and smiled, gleefully he recognized his kin.

"Daddy!" The squeal was one of infantile delight.

As Mark lifted the child and planted an abundance of tiny kisses about his face, Sally took me by the hand and pulled me close, kissing me on the cheek.

"Thank you," she whispered. "Thank you both so very, very much."

And then they were gone. There had been a momentary brightness, such as can be experienced during the heights of summer. A sudden cloud shift, allowing a burst of luminosity so bright as to be momentarily dazzling; then, just as rapidly, the clouds converge again and things return to as was. This is what we experienced in that moment, except there was no south facing window to account for the luminance which bathed the room. I blinked my eyes, attempting to re-adjust my vision to my surroundings.

"Is it over?" I asked Violet.

She swallowed, attempting to clear the lump which had built in her throat.

"Yes, Jack, we're done here."

"Good."

She could read the hope in my eyes. "This helped you find answers, to the other issue?"

"Yes. I can't be certain of the why or how of it, but I think I need to return to Foum Zguid, and as soon as is practical to do so."

"Jack?"

"Violet?" She was troubled.

"There was something else here."

"There was?"

She nodded sternly. "Something deeply unpleasant."

"Is it still here?"

"I don't think so. I can't feel it anymore."

"Then let's hope this is the end of things."

Violet looked far more pensive than was usual. "I'm sure this place is clean."

"Then why so glum?"

"It's nothing. I guess I was just brooding over my aunt."

"That's to be expected."

"I know… and it's good to know this home is at peace now."

I nodded. "I think it's time we got out of here."

We made our way through the hall, towards the front door; I rubbed a hand across the back of my neck. The fact I ached so, it was hardly surprising given recent events. Any abundance of tension tends to affect my body adversely, but currently it felt like my shoulders were weighed down carrying a sack full of rocks.

Violet stopped at the end of the path, turning and pointing to the flowered borders. "It might be worth your suggesting to Marcus they get this whole plot raked over. Nothing we can do about the place standing beside a bed of slate, but it'd be a sound idea to remove as much magnetite as possible. It's not a healthy mix, especially for anyone wishing to keep portals closed.

"It'll be top of my agenda when next I speak to Marcus," I said. "Now, can we leave? I'm more than done spending time at Misty Ridge."

Sixteen

That night, as I lay in bed listening to the relaxed rhythm of Linda's breathing, enjoying the intimacy of her limbs straddling my body, I decided it had been a wise decision. Listening to Violet, *forgetting* to inform my wife about this intended course of action, it was for the best. Her soft and regulated breathing helped only confirm that our safe return from Misty Ridge – amid self-proclamations of remarkable achievement – had allowed Linda's (and my mother's) anxieties to subside, thankfully moving us on past the horrors of previous days. Though I doubted either my wife or I could ever truly forget.

Nevertheless, Linda had endured enough worry these last hours. I had no wish to expand any disquiet. To the best of my knowledge, the first time I experienced *traveling* was on the night I almost died. Although further research has since guided me to believe this may not necessarily have been the case. Out-of-body experiences are apparently more common than is realized, although studies suggest these events are often discarded as simply being weird dreams, or else fade in their entirety from memory, upon waking. I have read upwards of two-dozen books, some dealing with the causality of these instances, and others offering valid trigger techniques aimed at activating the release of one's etheric body.

Untangling myself from Linda's embrace, I edged a gap between us and returned to lying on my back. According to a number of Eastern belief systems, the body contains several spiritual centers, or chakras. These chakras serve as focal ports, as storage centers for our energy fields, node points connecting our various vital – *subtle* – bodies, and as such can be used to gain access to higher realms, into different levels and realities. In theory, and with regular training, stimulation of these centers should allow instantaneous movement away from the physical form. Currently, however, this is not as yet a given with me. Although I have found that spending several minutes before bed, working through a set of predetermined techniques, it more often than not results in my experiencing a journey outside the physical body.

I closed my eyes, relaxing my limbs and listening for the sound of my heartbeat, feeling its rhythm, allowing each beat to expand through me. Every outwards pulse exponentially greater than the previous; allowing the beat to consume my form, every part merging, becoming one whole, until my body was my heart – my heart my body. I remained focused on this unified rhythm for several minutes, until I was absolutely certain that switching attention would not disrupt the regulated pulse of my existence. Then I switched focus to my fingers and toes; imagining these digits as roots of a tree. I visualized the energies of the universe flowing through these stems, flooding my body with vim, washing away the rigor of physicality, loosening the shackles of restraint on my subtle body, and then guiding these same energies to fill the cup of each chakra; charging life's batteries in order to drive the release. After several minutes spent meditating on these thoughts, I switched attention to a point behind my eyes, allowing my consciousness to sink into the treacle mattress of my skull; deeper and deeper still, all the while accepting, welcoming the realization I was slipping towards a different realm of existence.

She stands there, Aya, beside one of two domed windows set along the far wall; each opening gifts a panoramic over the town of Foum Zguid. The room is of Moorish design, with several recesses set beneath horseshoe arches, and with color and décor that is primarily white. Several hardwood beams strut the vault ceiling, their varnished tan contrasting nicely with white hanging shades. A line of pale recliners complement the room's overly achromatic tone. The floor is laid in tiles of Tangier Blue, but even these offer an abundance of pure and neutral color. An antique apothecary stands against the side wall; its aged frame painted lavender, thus barely contravening the alabaster theme.

Aya turns from the window and it is not without some surprise I realize she sees me. She speaks, and although her words remain foreign to me, her eyes plead urgency.

"I don't understand what it is you need."

She repeats words previously spoken.

I shake my head and show my palms to indicate I am at a loss. "I'm sorry," I say, and immediately realize the meaning of my words is just as lost.

A desperate babble of Moroccan Arabic follows as Aya turns and moves swiftly towards the arched doorway, gesturing that I trail behind her. Though I do not understand the words, still it is clear she begs my help. We move along the same wide hallway I have traversed on a number of previous occasions. At the end of the hallway is a wide spiral staircase, and as we begin the ascent I am overcome with dawning realization, and equally sickening déjà vu. By the time Aya reaches the door at the end of the landing I am left with little doubt as to what comes next, even though I still fail to understand my purpose as witness. She turns and faces me, checking my eyes for confirmation I will not flee this scene virtually upon us. I nod affirmation. She pushes the door ajar, and I follow her into the bathroom.

The bath is filled almost to brimming, the water riding gently into the forest of Mehdi's chest hair. Laid back in the water, eyes closed, he rests the nape of his neck on the rim of the tub. His olive features clearly showing a strain previous visits had failed to recognize. I wonder how I could have been so blind, so wrapped up by the awe of my astral traveling; I had failed to understand the misery overhanging this home.

It is then I notice the glint of silver, a flash of steel beneath subdued overhead lighting, and finally all becomes clear. Laid on the edge of the bath, most of its length hidden beneath the flat of Mehdi's right hand, a cutthroat razor awaits its calling. For one flickering moment I consider the possibility I am wrong, that Mehdi's sole intention is the careful tidying of his beard; but Aya's tone has returned to frantic, and one look into her eyes tells me all I must do.

Mehdi lifts the blade, carefully examining its edges before his eyes.

Taking hold of Aya's hand, I guide her towards the side of the tub, gently encouraging that she places her palm atop Mehdi's wrist. He doesn't sense her presence, and remains oblivious to her touch as he continues eyeing the cold steel. Her eyes plead with frantic desperation, and for a reason that escapes me, I experience an epiphany. I place hands on the pair of them, touching each at the shoulder, and as I fulfill my role as a conduit of reunion, he sees her.

Mehdi releases the blade, and with a soft plink it disappears beneath the bathwater. A babble of words escape him as his face streams tears...and understanding begins to wash over me, amid a mounting tide of awareness.

"Forgive me, Mehdi," she says.

Do I truly understand the words, or just the sentiment of their intent?

"I don't understand. How can this be possible?" Mehdi repeats the same question over and again.

Aya brushes away his tears with the backs of her fingers. "I had to find a way to stop you from committing this sin for which I am surely accountable. You must not; you have a life to live, my darling Mehdi."

He plants little kisses over the hand at his face. "I was such a fool, Aya. Those things I said. The things I did. I took my pain out on you. Forgive me, my love."

She leans in and gently kisses his lips. "Of course I forgive you. I have always loved you, Mehdi. I always will."

"How is this possible, my wife?" he asks, and then, for the first time seems to realize my presence; he starts, splashing back in the water, in such a manner I may well have just appeared from out of thin air. "In the name of God... is this visitor an angel?"

I smile at the absurdity of such a thought.

"I'm not sure what he is, my husband, but he may well be."

I shake my head. "I'm no angel."

I see Mehdi's jaw clench. "What then? Djinn? A devil?"

A change of tack is needed. As strange as all of this is for me, I recognize that for a devout man such as Mehdi, reunion with one's dead wife pushes the barriers of extreme. "I am neither devil nor djinn, and neither do I claim to be an angel from God. But I am here to do His work. So, rest assured, my friend, my purpose is to help."

"A fool such as I is beyond God's help."

"Do not ever think that, my husband. Isn't it through His hand that I am here to stay your actions?"

Our words and manner seem to reassure him somewhat. He returns his attention to Aya, who weeps over joyous reunion. "Stall your tears, my love. Soon our pain will be over, and we will spend eternity together under the grace of Allah."

She pulls back from his embrace. "No! This is not the way. Look at me, Mehdi. I am cursed. There is no place in Heaven for a sinner such as I, and if you persist with this, likely no place for you, either."

"Then I will bleed my wrists, and we will walk an eternity in shadow, together."

"No! Foolish man! You have life to live. When your time comes I shall be waiting, and if He sees fit to forgive my sin, and if you should see fit to forgive my failings as a wife and mother, then

mayhap we might yet spend an eternity together. But such stupid ideas and ideals ruining your thoughts, they present no opportunity; neither reunion nor salvation can be attained via this road. Stay your hand, my love."

Mehdi cups her face in his hands. "My darling wife, you think you ever needed ask for condonation? It is I who should be on my knees begging you to forgive my failings. And if Heaven's gates are destined to remain closed to you, then I shall walk forever at your side, wherever that journey takes us."

"You would forgive me, Mehdi?"

"Of course I would forgive you. Though there has never been need for absolution."

"And you promise to forget whatever silly notions now possess you?"

"Through my own foolishness I am obligated. I miss you so much."

"No, Mehdi! You are indeed a fool to speak such words. You must stop this madness. I miss you too, my husband. And I promise I will be waiting...but only when the time is right."

Mehdi dips his hand beneath the water and scoops up the razor, turning it over in his hands, inspecting it almost lovingly, intimately, until finally he places it on the edge of the tub. I had not until this point realized it was possible for a face to display such a cluster of emotions, the absolute joy of finding true love returned, and the gut wrenching, soul destroying realization of one you love being forever beyond reach.

Mehdi's wet eyes grieve acceptance. "I light a candle for you each and every night, my darling, so that it may guide your way home to me. I shall find you, again. I promise this with all of my heart."

Aya leans closer to kiss him. "I love you too, my husband," she says, and then turns to me. "And thank you, my angel, for this thing you have done. But I must beg of you one last favor. And it is only that you help me kee –"

Before she can finish addressing me, the inexplicable happens. We are thrown into darkness as the room turns to cold obsidian, an act followed almost immediately by the flaring of an encompassing aura – its sole purpose seemingly to identify where Aya stands. It is as though I am standing on a winter darkened street as someone opens a door, a disquietingly familiar backdrop of red lighting – somber and dull, yet tremendous in its glare – silhouetting Aya's form against the cold and misty night. In that one starburst moment I see both confusion and fear in her eyes, and for a moment I think I spy another figure, something with pink skin and a flattened snout, moving huge and foreboding over her shoulder, its muscled, white haired arm stretching round her waist... and then she is gone, swallowed amid a red-hued wave of gloom and desolation.

Without fully comprehending what I have seen, I feel sick to the core of my soul. Whatever fate just befell the woman remains unproven, though doubtless it seems one that is daunting; because, although I saw great concern afflicting her, and regardless of what my own eyes beheld; for the first and only time since I learned to access this state of being, the condition of peaceful tranquility which accompanies all of my travels, it was washed away by the tide of foreboding and wretchedness accompanying Aya's departure. Within those next few moments, even before I have any true opportunity to begin dissecting whatever it is has happened I begin to feel another all too familiar pull. I am about to be yanked across the void, physicality beckoning a swift return. The universe – or some force of it – indicating it is through with my services for this night, and for once, as I stand overcome by sadness beyond reasoning, I am pleased by the prospect of an imminent departure and my return to the corporeal.

"What happened? Where is Aya? Where did she go?" Mehdi pleads these same questions over and again.

My lips quiver to a forced smile, and I achieve a miniscule of comfort with the knowledge he seems not to have witnessed that which I saw. The pull grows stronger, and although I know I am short on time, still I attempt assurances with my lies. "God forgives, Mehdi. God forgives, all."

Relief scratches his face. "The angels, they have granted her passage?"

I point to the razor beside the bath. "You heard your wife's words. Do not stain your soul with that thing."

His eyes flick to the blade then as quickly return to me, and he nods knowingly. He understands, and I hold a smile as I meet his damp eyes, they are an ocean contaminated with grief. I tell myself it is a good thing we have achieved here this night, staying Mehdi's hand, and for this I am thankful. Though I have neither mettle nor heart enough to tell him, whatever it was claimed Aya, I feel sure it was no representative of their deity; and for certain, nothing angelic.

Seventeen

I have barely slept these last few nights. More than seventy-two hours have passed, yet I am still plagued by the circumstances of those events in Foum Zguid. For a long period following my accident, my memory retention had the consistency of soup...oh, how I wish I could so easily forget these last days.

I know what I saw, though still I find myself having moments of self-doubt, wondering perhaps if I am guilty of embellishing occurrences in Foum Zguid. Maybe, and it pains me to say this, I have been culpable of expanding the drama of not just that situation, but also those prior events at Misty Ridge...or is there some other reason I find it so difficult to believe? It is possible, and I cannot know this for sure, but is it not conceivable that, in the recent past my failing memory has actually been a mechanism for self protection? Although, if this is indeed the case, then why didn't my subconscious react this time, and banish all memories of Foum Zguid from my mind? It would certainly have been an aid to my mental welfare. *These terrible things I have seen...the horrors I have experienced.*

One satisfaction I do have, the things we achieved these past days, at least with regards to Misty Ridge, they have been good for all concerned. Violet explained to me that Mark's spirit had been trapped, unable to move on from the cottage. Firstly because of what had happened to his wife and child, and secondly because of the nature of his own demise. His poor soul being forced to constantly relive those dreadful rows with Sally, the pain of losing both wife and child, and finally the taking of his own life; suffering a lonely, bloody death submerged beneath carmine waters. I rubbed a hand across the back of my neck. The tension there seems to weigh even heavier now than before.

I think once more of the Featherstones, and of how strange it is to think their essences remained locked in such close proximity; being forced to indulge in ghostly arguments, perhaps on an almost daily basis. Played out by the ethereal energies imprinted on their home, and yet some indefinable – though unquestionably cruel – force kept their actual spirits, their souls, from coming together and finding peace.

The Stauntons didn't return to Misty Ridge until almost twenty-four hours had elapsed following our *cleansing* of the cottage; instead they'd opted to accept an offer of overnight accommodation with sympathetic friends. Things had reached a stage where any opportunity offering them absence from the property seemed like a Godsend, and so, when finally they plucked up courage to return, they had been staggered by the atmosphere now layering their home.

Faye told me they had spent much of the previous day and night discussing their options. Selling up and moving from Misty Ridge would have proved a financial burden. Nevertheless, they decided a move was their preference, and possibly their only option for retaining some sanity. The events they had witnessed, particularly those in the bedroom, it had proven too much for them to cope with.

And yet, upon returning, they felt instantly that things would be different now. Both Marcus and Faye claimed to feel an aura of peace and tranquility settled upon the place. Even young Peter seemed happier; content to toddle off and play alone, no longer expressing a need to keep his parents close by, in order for him to remain settled. Whatever the dark presence Violet detected at Misty Ridge, it would seem her actions succeeded in removing it. Another bizarre offshoot to this case, since concluding our business at the cottage, I have begun to recover some sensation down my right side. It's weird, but I have even managed to move about the house minus a cane, at least on occasion. I should be feeling ecstatic, but I wish I could shake the sense of unease still troubling me. Aya's fate is a mystery, and likely will remain so... Truly though, I fear for her soul.

Violet, as usual, proved her worth as an invaluable asset, and in all honesty, without her help in this case, as with so many others; I would have been totally out of my depth. It was she who offered me some pointers before I made a return to Foum Zguid.

Violet has been saying for a long time now, my defying death that night on the motorway, she feels I am here to serve some *higher purpose*. I can't honestly say I'm convinced of this – and even less so now, given how events played out – but the way I was able to conduit between Aya and Mehdi, this had at least given me food for thought. As too, sadly, does the way Aya met her end, if that is indeed what transpired. Violet seems as much at a loss as I, but I can tell she was troubled by my recounting of these events; though I guarantee not as distressed as I.

Violet insisted I should take faith in the knowledge there is something beyond this existence, and that, as of yet, our investigations haven't even begun to scratch the surface. My worry though, I fear I may have glimpsed some of what lies beyond, and it fills me with nothing but dread.

Despite my earlier promise of clarity, I declined giving Linda the full details of how Foum Zguid played out. She doesn't deserve further worry. And, of course, she is now more insistent than ever that my psychic sidekick accompanies me on *all* future escapades. I wonder if she would feel the same if Violet was twenty five years old and fitted a dress size eight? Somehow I doubt it.

Still, my darling wife was glad to get me back from the Staunton home in one piece, and even more relieved she didn't wake up next to my cold, rigidly catatonic body – the idea of my continued astral traveling, it terrifies her. And, truth to tell, at this moment it terrifies me. I foresee problems on that horizon…and I don't need to be psychic to predict them, either.

Linda suggested cooking up something special for dinner tonight; a reward for jobs well done. I figured this'd be a good idea, giving us the chance to relax and to turn our thoughts away from things otherworldly; even if only for a short while. I was hoping she'd be putting a nice corn-beef tart in the oven, and perhaps that would be followed by an early night and a couple of rest days.

I knew it would be important I try and get some rest, because next week is looking interesting. First thing Monday morning, Violet and I are traveling down to Wales. Local news channels are reporting a young woman has been arrested following a number of brutal slayings, and she faces charges of triple homicide. A fourth man is battling for survival in intensive care. I think it fair to say, he may be in no condition to think straight. Nevertheless, he claims that just prior to the woman committing her crimes; he witnessed her shape-shift into the form of a panther. It brings back that one resolute memory from my childhood. *Perhaps life really is an oceanic ball of possibilities, and, given enough time, history does retread old ground.*

I was drawing up the closing lines of these case files, while also contemplating whether Linda had started preparing lunch. I'm thinking it might make a nice change for us to eat out, when suddenly I hear Linda calling up the stairs. She insists I hurry down and join her. Urgency afflicts her cry, as does a level of stress suggesting a matter requiring immediate attention.

I find her downstairs in the lounge, arms wrapped tightly across her chest as she stands scrutinizing a breaking news report. A stern faced young woman talks directly into the camera. A red ribbon displays across the bottom of the television screen, presenting regularly rotated captions, banner headlines identifying aspects of the travesty taken place. My eyes follow the latest stream of words: *Breaking News: Hundreds Feared Dead in Paris Attack: Passenger Aircraft Strikes Eiffel Tower.*

Another caption flashes onscreen identifying the ashen faced reporter as Sofie Reyes. The girl looks barely old enough to be out of school, and yet she laments with media practiced contrition, as over her shoulder a backdrop of beacons flash atop a multitude of emergency vehicles.

I turn and address my wife. "Jesus. Did this just happen?"

"Just keep watching, Jack," Linda says, her eyes betraying the fact there is more to this than I am yet aware of.

My eyes flick back to the television, and a box opens in the top corner of the screen showing ground level footage of what has occurred. The handheld camera captures the precise moment when, at 11.30am local time, Moroccan Airlines flight 743 strikes the upper tier of the tower, shearing of the top third of the lattice structure. As the wrought iron of the upper tier separates from the main frame, it seems to momentarily hover before freefalling towards the ground with the velocity of a gargantuan javelin. For a moment the plane sits perched atop the broken tower, its breached hull snagged by struts of ruptured steel, but an explosion within the aircraft causes it to blow apart, its burning tail and nose falling away either side of the building. As fire rages atop the lattice, teardrops of heat cry down through the structure, igniting the middle tier restaurant area; a further explosion follows, and as flames lick and claw the center section of the tower, it is impossible not to recognize there is humanity among the charred remnants falling from this area.

"Oh my God," I whisper. "This is awful." I slip my arm round Linda, though I know this small action will not halt the flow of her tears.

"It gets worse," she whispers, and I look at her quizzically. "Keep watching. This whole broadcast is on rinse and repeat. Just keep watching."

She has barely finished before the screen changes, switching to a somber faced duo back in the studio.

"Do we have any further news on motive or culpability, yet, Jackie?" laments the fifty-something desk-jockey, his hands clasped in rehearsed penitence.

"Well, Tom, French authorities have just released this latest update. They believe upwards of a thousand tickets had already been issued granting access to the Eiffel Tower, prior to Manchester bound Moroccan Airlines flight 743 striking the building. The aircraft was believed to be carrying 234 passengers, plus a crew of eleven. It is also being reported there were heavy numbers of tourists in the ground level vicinity of the tower at the time of the attack.

"Authorities have confirmed the validity of a recording issued by Islamic Shield, in which a man, dressed in a Moroccan Airline's flight uniform, addresses the issues of constant infringements by Western governments into Middle Eastern affairs – the image of a sanguine featured individual in a pilot's uniform flashes onscreen, and as the man talks directly into the camera, my heart sinks – *Authorities have identified the speaker as Mehdi Harrak, a 36-year-old widower, who has been employed for the last six years as a pilot with Moroccan Airlines. Unconfirmed reports have suggested Harrak may have been scheduled to take charge of today's flight 743, Marrakech to Manchester..."*

The reporter's words continued on but they were lost to me as the reality of what was unfolding almost dropped me to my knees. I was crushed by the realization of having so misread these past weeks.

The clues had been there, but I had chosen to miss them. The guests I observed visiting the house in Foum Zguid. I had at first assumed they were there for a dinner party, or some other social gathering. Later on, once I learned the truth about Aya's demise, it seemed likely they were concerned family members, there to offer support to Mehdi.

I think of poor Aya, and of her husband turning from her following the loss of their child. She showed me how he had been spending ever more time away, seeking solace at prayer with newfound friends. Was it these people who could have influenced such a mindset? As I recall the sadness I saw in Aya's eyes the night those people sat at her table, I cannot help but wonder over the true reasons behind their visiting Mehdi in his time of grief.

What a fool I have been. Aya's pleas that I help stay her husband's actions; I had assumed she referred to his using the blade. Of course she wanted him to go on living. She had no desire for him to end his own life, but it was the greater evil he had been pressured towards, it was this she hoped I could sway him from. Her final unfinished sentence, she had begged my help to stay his hand...and then she had been taken.

The muscles in my face tighten. It feels as though a weight is pressing down through the top of my skull, squishing my brain, compressing my spine. I recall my mother's words. *We are all just pawns being played. And you, my boy, there is a higher power seeking to make use of you.*

For a moment I felt as though I would faint, but thankfully I stayed on my feet. Was it really possible I had been used as a pawn in some cosmic game? And to what end? The events at Misty Ridge already seemed unlikely, the coincidences even more so. Sally Featherstone had been able to seek my help purely because I now lived in a house formerly owned by her parents. I'd assumed I had been pulled towards Foum Zguid simply because there was a similarity to the tragedies suffered; creating a conduit of pain that opened a connection between the Featherstone and Harrak families.

But was I always, in reality, simply being guided?

Perhaps not by anything with an intention, or even any interest in resolving the Featherstone's plight, but rather I was there solely to ensure Aya found no way of staying her husband's actions. Sure enough, I was allowed to prevent him using the razor, and that likely was the very reason for my being there. *Something* needed to ensure Mehdi didn't step away from his designated path. Aya was taken before she could make me understand the true purpose for which he had been chosen. My dissuading Mehdi from suicide, it had felt so good; a personal triumph. But my good deed had cost the lives of hundreds, maybe thousands.

"Are you ok, Jack?" Linda's attention had drifted from the TV screen and was now focused on me, but I couldn't bring myself to respond to her question.

Even with all of the trials I've endured over these last few years, my wife isn't used to seeing me in tears. I wondered if perhaps my mother had been right all along, and we are all but peons allotted roles in some cruel and dreadful pastime. I closed my eyes, only to be greeted by the pale-skinned nightmare still haunting me. And although the curl of Her lips pretenses into a smile, it fills me with dread when I look into Her black eyes, and realize She is not yet done with me.

Humankind is but the pieces in a game, plastic soldiers waging war between boy gods.

A Basis for Misty Ridge: And a Truth Stranger than Fiction

As a young child I used to believe that every adult male started work just after 4am, and that it was normal for families to move home regularly (at least once every twelve months); I also believed ghosts were real.

I was raised in the shire town of Northampton, in the very heart of England. My parents worked hard all their lives. Dad putting in long shifts at the Watney Mann brewery – six mornings a week, just a couple of minutes after 4am, light would bleed under the bedroom door and alert me to the fact my father would shortly be embarking on a fifteen minute bicycle ride to his place of work. Mother would busy herself throughout the day, looking after my sister and me, doing chores and prepping the evening meal, and then, once Dad returned from the brewery, Mum (Mom to my American friends) would head off out to do cleaning rounds at a local factory.

Dad would tidy up the dinner plates, then spend time keeping us amused before getting us ready for bed, and finally he'd read to us until Mum got back and gave us our "goodnight" cuddles. I still have fond memories of my early years and those bedtime stories, and I credit my parents' willingness to engage us in such tales, as doubtless the spark for where I now find myself.

There are no great reveals in these opening lines, plenty of families have to cover rotating shifts in order to place food on the table and meet their bills. However, I didn't realize it at the time (how could I have?) but my parents were working towards a plan. They were grafting like Trojans in order to raise funds for investment in bricks and mortar. Once my sister and I started school, the parental roster changed. Mum took a day job fitted around school hours – a necessity in order to free up some time in the evenings – and they used the savings they had set aside to fund our move to a slightly larger home; albeit one requiring extensive modernization. This quickly became the norm. My parents would buy a rundown property, and fitting life around our schooling and their regular jobs, they would work long hours into the evenings and weekends readying the place for occupation. We'd then move in, and they would carry out the more superficial decorating tasks while our previous residence was sold off. Then the whole process would begin anew, and in less than a year we would likely be packing our belongings into boxes, once again.

My parents worked hard to make sure they balanced becoming financially stable with keeping a roof over our heads, and perhaps it is only looking back now I can truly appreciate just how much effort they put in.

I was eight years old when my parents discovered what they believed would be our dream home. Myrtle House stood abandoned and derelict on the outskirts of Kingsthorpe village. The once impressive sandstone cottage had been standing empty for almost fifty years, and now offered little more than a two-hundred year-old shell. There weren't even any useable stairwells remaining with which to access the two upper levels. The place was in need of *serious* renovation. Unlike with a majority of the projects my parents had previously taken on, we kids weren't even allowed anywhere near the site. In fact, a blanket ban remained over the renovation for several months. The potential for hazard deemed too great.

Eventually we moved into the semi-completed building, which now existed as a five-bedroom home, covering three levels. Although an impressive structure, Myrtle House was no mansion. Nevertheless, for two kids who started life in a small terrace, on the edge of Northampton Boroughs, a home of this grandeur was impressive.

Even once we moved in there remained a further year of solid graft before my parents were reasonably content with their labors.

Already things seemed *not quite right*. We owned a lurcher named Blackie (perhaps not the best choice of name when looking back, but, hey, it was the early 1970s, and that's the originality you get when you allow a six-year-old David Brian to name your dog). I loved that black dog, he was my best friend.

But the bundle of fun and energy that was Blackie, he was never happy at Myrtle House. He would constantly whine to be let outside, and eventually all but lived in the conservatory attached to the rear of the property. He would come inside in the evenings to sit with us beside the open fireplace, but even before we retired for bed he would move back into *his* conservatory. The property was on three levels, but Blackie would cry if you called for him to join you upstairs. This was a dog who could jump a five-foot fence, and who, in our previous homes, had always enjoyed sitting at the top of the stairs, his paws overhanging the step as he surveyed his domain.

But not at Myrtle House.

Even during that first year objects would move unaided, inexplicably falling off shelves, sliding from table-tops, or bins and buckets would upend themselves on the floor. These things were laughed of by my dad, often attributed to draughts blowing through open windows, or the thumping beat of a radio having vibrated ornaments, books or cutlery from wherever they had been displaced.

We children weren't convinced.

And neither was our mother.

Truth to tell, I'm fairly certain my dad didn't believe his own explanations, either. It was likely that his primary concern when coming up with these excuses was being not to unsettle the rest of the family. It didn't work. We three were certain something else existed within the borders of our home (and I'm convinced Blackie believed the same). Numerous odd things happened, including a stack of magazines, newspapers, and books that lifted itself several inches in the air, before moving horizontally away from the table and then slumping to the ground without displacing even one object from the gathered pile. (This happened one evening as our whole family sat gathered around the TV.)

We began to catch glimpses of a woman, who would occasionally smile before moving on or disappearing from sight – she looked to be around forty years of age, which at that time of my life seemed *really* old. She wore a close-fitting dress; the dark outfit being reminiscent of those I've seen in Victorian photos featuring everyday wear from the 1870/80s.

Our resident ghost(s) became a family joke (even among more widespread family members), but things took a dark turn. I walked up the stairs one evening, and as I turned onto the landing I was confronted by the ghostly woman standing directly in front of me. I was terrified. This wasn't some snatched glimpse of a shadowy figure, but rather she was close enough, real enough to be an intruder in our home; an intruder dressed for a costume party. Furthermore, the look of shock and horror on the woman's face, she hadn't expected to see me on *her* landing. I have often pondered this, those earlier sightings of this smiling figure, were they just images pulled from another time; perhaps images of her smiling at someone else – or sometime else?

Shortly after this we attended a family gathering on the other side of Northampton. While we were away Blackie somehow managed to unlock the conservatory door and flee from the house. His escape entailed scaling a six-foot wall, and he died that night after being struck by a car as he ran towards the open pastures of Kingsthorpe Mill.

Losing him was this small boy's first experience of heartbreak. More bad things were to follow. Just a week after losing Blackie, my mum was standing on tippy-toes adjusting a curtain rail in one of the upstairs bedrooms. Somehow she managed to upend herself, crashing down face-first onto the recessed shelf of the window ledge. She ended up with an eye swollen to resemble a blue-black egg, and thirty-nine stitches in a head wound. She claimed to have fallen because someone had grabbed her ankles and upended her, and all while she was being treated her protestations never ceased. It was a bizarre thing; those unaccountable bruises around ankles, they certainly resembled finger marks.

We had lived there for coming up on five years, but finally the house was placed on the market; we children being under strict instruction to remain quiet about any of the unsettling goings on. It was a fine looking property, and it sold for a healthy sum relatively quickly. We moved on to a new home some miles away, and everything there was rosy.

As an aside, about a year after we moved out of Myrtle House, a friend of mine started dating the daughter of the family who had bought the property. One afternoon the girl approached me, and in a somewhat hesitant manner asked if *anything strange* had ever happened while we were living at the house? I remembered the oath of secrecy to which I had been sworn, and so answered 'no.' I didn't even ask why she was asking such a thing, lest I open a can of worms. Not engaging her on the subject of that house, it is something I regret to this day.

As a young child I believed every adult male started work just after 4am, and that it was perfectly normal for families to move home at least once every twelve months. I no longer believe such things to be true.

Final Thoughts

Way back in 2002 I wrote a ghostly tale titled *The Strange Case at Misty Ridge,* and it is fair to say that aspects of that short story were inspired by my childhood and events at Myrtle House.

The story was published in 2013, appearing in *Kaleen Rae And Other Weird Tales.* In 2016 I decided to open things up and to expand on the original tale, but without writing to any pre-plotted guidelines. The novel you have just read is the end result of those endeavors.

I should like to take this opportunity to offer up a huge and genuine thank you to everyone who has taken time to read *The Strange Case at Misty Ridge.* We writers can be an insecure bunch, so thank you for the continuing support and words of encouragement. It is greatly appreciated.

I hope you have enjoyed this book. If so, then please consider sparing a few minutes to post a review on Amazon.com, or any other relevant sites. Reviews offer a valuable source of exposure for authors, and this is especially true for writers in the indie community.

Best wishes.

David Brian.

If you enjoyed this book, then you may be interested in these other titles:

The Boy on the Beach

As Juliet stepped down from the last step onto the damp sand beneath her feet, she said a silent prayer to the Lord that He hadn't allowed the old staircase to fail her. The way its metal frame groaned as she descended the steps, she had been all but convinced it was on the verge of collapse. Now though, standing on the cool sand, a warm breeze blowing in from the ocean gently caressing her face, she was stunned by the majesty of her surroundings.

The beach was in the shape of a crescent bordered all around by a sprawling wall of black rock. Against this blackness Juliet could make out several areas of even greater darkness painted onto the rock face. She realized these huge voids were the openings to caves, carved out of the rocks by the pounding ocean over the course of thousands of years. This part of the British coastline was renowned for these features. In front of her the ocean crashed mercilessly against majestic giants which rose in columns from the sea bed. She watched fascinated as the dark waters turned to white spray under the behemoth's solid stance.

Eventually she stepped forward, slowly at first, but then her stride quickened until she found herself running at top speed across the sand toward the breaking ocean.

She laughed joyfully as she stepped knee high into the cool waters and a sudden spray of foam splashed upwards hitting her full in the torso, upending her, sending her sprawling with an almighty splash, onto her back. Juliet shuddered, just for an instant as the cold ocean caressed warm skin, and then she once again laughed as she began to thrash her arms and legs through the water, supplying herself with just enough buoyancy to stay afloat in the shallows.

As she drifted, looking up at the moon overhead, which still continued its peak through breaking clouds, Juliet realized this was the happiest she had felt in years. It was a revelation that painted sad condemnation on her young life.

Juliet lay in the shallow waters, her limbs providing a modicum of movement, though enough to deny the current's repeated attempts to beach her. Eventually she closed her eyes, intent on enjoying the sounds of the night. Somewhere distant, even over the steady beat of the waves playing onto the rocks, she could hear the penetrating call of a Nightjar. The wind seemed to whisper as it gently caressed her face and then rustled across the shoreline. She smiled to herself, marveling at the tranquility offered up by these various soothing rhythms. It was a long time before she realized there were other sounds being carried through the night.

Juliet stopped floating on her back. Rising to her feet she listened carefully, unsure of what it was she was trying to identify. The splashing of the waters against her legs was making it impossible to narrow down the direction the noise was coming from. She waded through the surf and back up the beach, immediately aware that her body temperature was dropping uncomfortably.

The ocean's caress was becoming a cool mistress.

Juliet shuddered as the breeze, which minutes earlier seemed so warming, now carried a chilling bite through the night air. She gripped the end of her nose between finger and thumb, and then attempted to breathe out through her nose in an effort to clear her ears of water. She tilted her head to one side, as people so often do when straining to hear something, and listened intently. It wasn't so much a discernable sound as a distant mantra borne on the night air. Maybe whispered voices, maybe music; Juliet couldn't be sure?

As she looked back up the beach, toward the iron staircase which she earlier descended, Juliet's attention was drawn towards the large black cavern away to her right. The opening to the cave looked huge, like the hungry mouth of a night monster waiting to devour her. For the first time Juliet felt uneasy, realizing just how alone she was; alone, and in the middle of nowhere. Of one thing she was now certain; the noise, it was coming from within the cave.

The Damnation Game

Joel Miller sat in one of the alcove booths. He took a swig of lager and then placed the drink down on the table, never once taking his eyes off the two people at the bar. Every few minutes, the big fella glanced in Joel's direction, aware that the figure in the booth was watching them with interest. Joel knew the black guy's name was Merrick and, apparently, he was more than capable of handling himself. He recognized the woman, too. Her name was Kate Stringer. Six months ago the murder of her 'have a go hero' husband had made big headlines. Initially it only broke as a local story, seeming like a street assault gone wrong. But the crime had soon been tied in to the Catholic Jack killings, and then the story had made the nationals.

Kate was sitting with her back to Joel, and yet her mannerisms and movement plainly demonstrated she was a woman in turmoil. Earlier, when he'd first arrived at the pub, he stood next to her at the bar. She was touching thirty but still an attractive woman. Even through her recent angst she had retained good looks. He would liked to have spoken with her, offered his condolences for a loss suffered. But how the hell do you broach that sort of conversation? Besides, she had been oblivious to his presence. Nevertheless, what had happened had been a travesty, and he intended doing all he could to resolve this woman's suffering.

Carmilla: The Wolves of Styria

A letter written by Doctor Alvinci, addressed to Baron Vordenburg. Dated *August 10th, 1860*

Dear Baron Vordenburg,

I write in the hope that you will remember meeting my good self; we were introduced at a garden party at the home of the Baroness von Waxensteini, almost three years ago.

It may help your memory of me if I tell you that I am a rather tall individual, standing several inches higher than the average Austrian male, a fact which you yourself commented on. The two of us spent some hours in conversation, in part because it became apparent that we shared a number of similar interests, particularly in all subjects esoteric. Things, that if I might say, you are substantially more adept at than myself. Although I should also mention that since last we spoke I have had experience of what I believe to have been a revenant, and unfortunately that incident did not end at all well for the young lady involved. I can assure you that the situation, with which I am now confronted, far outweighs that which has gone before. It is for this very reason that I write you now, as I feel sure that your expertise is needed in order to cleanse this district of a most despicable evil.

I am myself new to this area, having only arrived a fortnight earlier, and that at the behest of my good friend and colleague Doctor Spielberg. He knew of my interest in the arcane and he hoped, vainly as it transpired, that I may have been able to resolve the growing unpleasantness which surrounds us.

I will tell you now some of the strange and repugnant happenings which have been afflicting these lands, in the hope that you may be able to offer some guidance as to how these matters should be proceeded with.

For several weeks now this district has been subjected to a most mysterious malady, one which for the most part, but not always, tends to afflict females and usually then being girls within a certain range of ages. I myself had only been here for a number of days, when Doctor Spielberg suggested that I accompany him on his rounds as he was due that morning to visit Analiese Dorner, she being the young wife of a local swineherd, Bruno.

Analiese had some days earlier, claimed to have woken from her sleep to find something heavy attached to her throat. She fought desperately to free herself, as she felt, in her words, "that the very life was being throttled out of her." Then, without any obvious reason, the fiend released her. Sitting upright, she saw a darkly dressed figure on the far side of the room, near the door. For one brief moment she thought that she saw a female face staring back at her from under the cowl, and just as quickly the apparition was gone. Analiese spent some minutes trying to wake her husband, a light sleeper, from his position on the bed beside her, but was unable to rouse him. And within just a short time, she felt a strange melancholy sweeping through her body, debilitating her strength, and she quickly lapsed into a deep, but fitful sleep.

Doctor Spielberg and I arrived at the Dorner's modest dwelling, at just past midday; a worried looking Bruno greeted us upon our arrival. After a brief conversation, in which he largely despaired at his wife's continuing decline, we followed him inside to where his bedridden wife lay.

I must confess to having been shocked. Analiese, although bereft of any powders, as would be expected for a woman of her standing, nonetheless, she was a creature of beauty, or at least it was plain to see that she once had been. A thick mop of brown hair, streaked with layers of blonde, adorned her crown and hung down over her shoulders. Her skin though had a pallid complexion, and though she smiled to acknowledge our arrival, her eyes remained dull and lifeless. I took hold of her wrist, to check her pulse, and found the touch clammy beyond reason. Analiese's heart beat steadily, although her breathing remained shallow. She had no fever. Neither did she suffer from any pockmarks, or other rashes elsewhere on her body. The only mark we did find was the tiniest blue bruise on her neck, at precisely the point where she described the strangulation as having commenced.

We questioned the woman at length, where upon Analiese described in detail how since that first night, she had continued to suffer bouts of extremely fitful sleep, which usually involved dreams of a disturbing nature. She seemed highly reluctant to elaborate on the qualities of these dreams, although I sensed a degree of embarrassment in her coyness, rather than the fear of being forced to relive her nightmares. At my behest, my colleague took notes while I interviewed the woman, as he later did when we visited others in the area who had been similarly afflicted.

In total we attended the care of four patients, thus infected, in my first week here. I have to say there was a marked degree of similarity in each case. Each of those questioned exhibiting the same lack of vigour, and pallid complexion. They are also, as one, reluctant to elaborate on the nature of their dreams that accompany this illness.

Earlier this week, on the morning that Analiese; dressed in a pale blue dress, with yellow stitching bordering the hems, was laid to rest, we attended the bedside of a young peasant girl named Katharina Bohm. A very sad case indeed given that the child was aged just sixteen years, even more so insofar as her father had raised her alone, the child's mother dying of fever some twelve years earlier.

Her papa, although reluctant to leave his sick child, had gained some work within the forest, and so had not returned home until after dark the previous night. Upon approaching their dwelling, the father heard his daughter moaning and calling out. Believing her to be in pain he strode out to their cottage, only to find upon entering, a most despicable sight. Something dark was astride the girl, its head buried into her chest. According to the peasant, his daughter was indeed crying out, though not as he had first thought in pain, but rather in a way more akin to a couple alone.

Upon his entrance the beast withdrew from the girl, snarling and spitting as it did so. It became apparent that the fiend was a woman, at least of sorts. The black cloak that covered it fell open, revealing a naked female body, although the things face was twisted into a visage more suited to a demon escaped from hell. The riding-hood seemed to move as though possessed of a life its own, shimmering and distorting as the she-fiend leapt from the bed. The peasant thought his life was done, but instead the creature, now on all fours, bounded past him, moving he thought with an element of gracefulness, like some gigantic cat. Turning back to his daughter, he was distraught to find her nightgown hoisted high around her waist, and the upper fastenings loosed and pulled down, exposing her naked breasts. He covered the girl, and then attempted to wake her, but she never once again opened her eyes. Katharina died in the early hours of yesterday morning.

In this correspondence to you, I shall include copies of all notes taken, and also medical assessments carried out by my colleague and I, in the hope that these things will help to illuminate an answer to this most grave matter. I have only ever read accounts of creatures such as the oupire, and succubus, hence I have no way of truly knowing if such demons can walk among us, although as you will have reasoned from my contacting you, I do consider this to be a likely explanation. Time is most certainly pressed in dealing with this situation, and I fear that without your expert guidance we may truly be lost. Therefore, I would beseech you to advise me forthwith as to how we may best proceed, in order that we are swiftly able to vanquish this onset of evil.

Sincerely yours,

Doctor Sebastian Alvinci.

23848279R00139

Printed in Great Britain
by Amazon